VELMA SCOTT & THE CURIOUS CASE OF THE TELEPATHISTS

WRITTEN BY:
Alex Stivaros

8TH & ATLAS PUBLISHING

8TH & ATLAS PUBLISHING

8th & Atlas Publishing
911 Walnut Street
Winston-Salem, NC 27101

www.8thandatlaspublishing.com

This book was ethically and responsibly manufactured by
Lightning Source.

This book was edited by Hana Kim, Michael De Paris, and
Christina De Paris

print ISBN: 978-1-7377181-8-5
ebook ISBN: 978-1-7377181-9-2

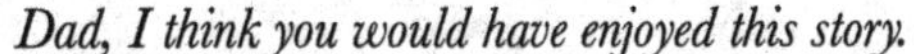

Dad, I think you would have enjoyed this story.

PROLOGUE

Shores of Loch Ness, Scotland, 1929...

The biting chill of the night air gnawed at their exposed skin. Undeterred, the hooded throng continued their torch-lit procession around the banks of the Loch. Overhead, the night sky was clear, and the moon cast a luminous, otherworldly glow over the dark, freezing waters. As their haunting chants echoed around its banks, the surface of the Loch gently ebbed.

Gradually, the procession came to a stop, and its devotees gazed adoringly over at their leader. He threw back his hood and grinned towards them with a stoic mania. Enthralled by his presence, they gasped as the light from their flaming torches reflected in the fiery glare of his eyes. He boomed, his voice clear and precise, "Tonight—is a very special night!" Widening his arms, he cajoled his eager flock around him. "My friends, tonight we summon the elemental forces surrounding us and ask for their assistance."

Breathless with anticipation, his congregation

surged forward and roared their approval. Their leader's gaze swung towards three small cloaked figures, who huddled fearfully amongst his coven. Pounding his fist rhythmically against his palm, he roared, "What we do tonight, we do for the sake of the world and for all of mankind."

His followers murmured their consent as the diminutive cloaked figures in their midst were thrust before the coven leader. He pointed ominously at the first, who removed his hood with trembling hands and sank fearfully to his knees. "Do you willingly accept the gift I am about to bestow?"

Shaking his head defiantly, the young boy's voice wavered as he answered, "No, I will not." Fearfully, the younger child beside the daring boy wailed as a hush descended over the coven; they were aghast at the youngster's act of defiance.

The coven leader solemnly considered his reply and then growled, "If that is your answer, boy, then another fate awaits you." He motioned with a long crooked finger towards the Loch and hissed, "Cast the disbeliever into the waters of the beast."

A look of fear crossed the child's face. He struggled helplessly as white hooded figures swarmed him, grabbing at his small-boned body and roughly trussing together his hands. Looming above the boy, the coven leader's blood red robe flowed regally behind him. He then knelt on one knee, besides the terrified, bound child.

Unwilling to meet his fierce gaze, the boy looked away and felt the coven leader's breath hot on his face. The sickly sweet smell made the boy want to vomit. Leaning closer, the coven leader placed his mouth close to the child's ear. Whispering harshly so that only the boy could hear him, he muttered a curse that caused the child to cry out.

Smiling with satisfaction, the coven leader rose to his feet and straightened his robes with long, slender fingers. Ashen-faced, the boy began to sob as the throng bayed deliriously with anticipation.

As the muted wails of the children carried into the night, the red-robed figure closed his eyes as though deep in prayer. After a brief moment passed, he nodded, with a barely perceptible movement of his head.

Strong hands fervently grabbed beneath the boy's arms and plucked him from the ground. Ignoring his protests, the enraptured assembly dragged him kicking and screaming over the rocks. Brittle and sharp, the terrain bit and gnawed at his legs, leaving crimson spots of blood in their wake as the crowd manoeuvred him towards the edge of the Loch. Struggling helplessly against their vice-like grip and unable to quell his impending sense of doom, the boy soiled himself.

Like the steady pounding of a drum, the mob's chanting grew louder as the boy was suspended in mid-air by a pair of strong hands. Howling with delirium, the coven eagerly watched on as the boy's body suddenly plunged headlong beneath the surface of the water.

The throng licked their lips with anticipation as the child was cast unrepentantly into the murky, freezing depths of Loch Ness. A reverential hush descended as they eagerly awaited the monstrous sight that was to be his fate...

ONE

London, England, May 12th, 1959

Douglas Salter buried his hands deep in his coat pockets as he hurried home from work. The sky was grey, almost charcoal, and heavy with dark clouds, which perfectly mimicked his melancholy mood. His heavy tweed suit was drenched from the torrential rain that lashed down around him. Miserably, he trudged along the pavement, his shoes squelching, as he sidestepped a large puddle.

A rumble of engine noise approached somewhere behind him, and he turned to look over his shoulder. The newspaper reporter sighed forlornly, as he watched his evening bus racing past. Muttering to himself in annoyance, Douglas cursed his editor for holding him up at work and held tightly onto his hat as he dashed after it.

His footsteps splashed wildly as he ran. Wheezing, Douglas stopped just short of the bus stop, and doubled over. His lungs felt as if they were about to burst. The bus pulled away, and grimly he watched it disappear into the distance as a roll of thunder sounded overhead.

Cursing, he opted to take a shortcut and headed down the steps at the far end of the footbridge. They were slippery from the rain, and he moved carefully as he worked his way down. The street lights overhead flickered as he descended. They fizzled momentarily and suddenly blinked off, plunging him into darkness. Douglas came to an abrupt stop.

His mood worsened as he felt along the rough stone of the surrounding wall. Cursing his misfortune, he gingerly took the last remaining steps and then stumbled as he reached the bottom. The reporter sighed wearily as he lay at the foot of the steps, limbs in a tangle.

Douglas picked himself up and wiped at the grime on his hands and sodden suit. The reporter's grazed palms stung, the skin shorn off as they brushed against the harsh woollen fibre. Swearing loudly, he took a hesitant step forward and discovered that he'd twisted or sprained his ankle. He winced and leant against the wall as he took in the path ahead. Bathed in shadows, the deserted cobbled street appeared long and foreboding.

As soon as he set off, the headlights of a stationary car unexpectedly blinked on. Douglas gasped with surprise, the glare was blinding. Squinting, he attempted to block them out with his hand, the driver revved the engine. Nervously, the reporter hobbled across the road, trying to ignore the pain in his ankle. The growl of engine noise grew menacingly. He glanced worriedly over his shoulder as the car slowly approached; it appeared to be following.

Uneasily, Douglas made his way along the street. To his left lay an embankment that ran parallel alongside the canal. He gripped tightly onto the railings that lined it as the car's headlights refocused their beam on him. Anxiously, he picked up his pace with large strides. He shook his head ruefully and thought to himself, *this is no time to get mugged, or worse.*

As the mechanical din of the engine grew louder, Douglas started to feel a rising sense of panic. Apprehensively, he looked back and flinched as the car hurtled towards him. Caught in its headlights, he vaulted the railings and tumbled headlong down the embankment.

The seconds ticked by before the sound of water lapping against the shore brought him to his senses. He felt nauseous, and his head was pounding. Groggily, Douglas dragged himself upright and tenderly prodded a large lump forming on the back of his head.

As he pulled his hand away, his fingers felt sticky. *Blood,* he realised dolefully. Somewhere above him, he could hear voices chattering. Fear crept in as he held his breath and waited.

It seemed like ages before the sounds began to dissipate. He sat slumped on the embankment, rocking himself back and forth. All alone and fearing for his life, Douglas Salter felt most vulnerable as he sat there in the dark...

TWO

She smiled expansively and invited Douglas to take the chair opposite hers. "Please take a seat, Mr. Salter. As you know, my name is Velma, Velma Scott. And as you're aware, I'm a private investigator. However, I must emphasise that I only take cases that interest me. So, if you feel that yours is something I'd find interesting, please continue. I imagine that's why you're here after all?"

Impatiently, Douglas Salter puffed out his cheeks. "If you could just skip the background, Miss Scott, I know very well who you are." The detective frowned at his tone as he sullenly took the seat offered.

In her dimly lit office, he appeared pale and gaunt. She imagined that he was in his early thirties. He had clear blue eyes and thinning, sandy-coloured hair. Worry lines burrowed deep into his brow as he cleared his throat.

He looks troubled, Velma thought, as she watched a sweat bead trickle down his face. *Possibly coming down with something*, she mused, revising her opinion as she studied the reporter's appearance more closely.

"Well, I've introduced myself, Mr. Salter. Why don't you do me the courtesy of doing the same? We can discuss the details of your case once we've gotten to know each other a little. I prefer to know something about a person beforehand. You see, it gives me a little context to work with. I'm sure you understand where I'm coming from?"

Douglas nodded as he crossed his legs, rearranging himself in the hard wooden chair. He took a deep breath, unsure where to start. What wasn't in question was that he needed help, he was desperate. Exhaling slowly, Douglas thought back to the events of the previous evening and shivered. He'd spent the whole day asking around, checking with friends and colleagues. And the detective facing him came highly recommended.

He guessed that she was in her mid-fifties. She was tall, dressed in a green cardigan, white blouse, and navy woollen skirt. Her eyes were a steely grey that matched the wiry metallic hue of her hair.

The private investigator wasn't cheap by any means, but she was apparently the best. After what had happened, Douglas suspected that he needed the best money could buy. Someone was out to get him. And after his recent brush with danger, he was more convinced of that than ever.

"Look, I'm not being paranoid," he began as he introduced himself. "But I believe that someone is trying to kill me. I'm a reporter for *The Evening Post*. I cover marriages, births, deaths—that sort of thing. I'm not a big shot investigative reporter. I don't cover the headline stories and to be honest, I really wouldn't know how. That's why this is all so baffling to me. I don't understand who out there wants me dead. Or why."

Velma got up from behind her rectangular mahogany desk and stretched her legs. Shoeless, her thick brown tights cushioned her steps as she ambled over to the window and parted the blinds. The streets below bustled as people raced from place to place. Squinting against the glare of the streetlights outside, Velma hurriedly closed the blinds. She had an aversion to bright light, a long-standing condition. That's why she preferred to work in the early evening or preferably at night.

"So, what you're telling me is that you've not offended anybody or ruffled any feathers due to your work?" The reporter shook his head, mystified. Velma nodded to herself, "I'll need to see copies of everything you've published over the last few months, alright?"

Douglas nodded, feeling a surge of relief. "Does that mean that you'll take my case?"

The detective smiled. "Mr. Salter. I spoke with one of your colleagues at the newspaper earlier today. Your editor and I worked together during the war and we chat from time to time. He called today and mentioned that he was concerned about one of his staff, tipped me off that you might make your way over. And well, judging by the state of you, it really looks like you could do with some help. So yes, I'll take the case."

The reporter laughed with relief. "Thank you so much, Miss Scott. I really don't know how I can thank you."

Velma chuckled, "Prompt payment usually helps, Mr. Salter. The rates I charge for late payments are absolutely criminal." Her shoulders shook as she enjoyed her own joke. Her chortle faded and the detective fixed her new client with a stern glare. "Now then, Mr. Salter, shall we start again? Why don't you begin by telling me the truth?"

The reporter froze, "I…erm…" he mumbled uncomfortably.

She padded over from the window and tutted as she leant over him. The scent of her harsh perfume brought a tear to the reporter's eyes. "If you really want my help, Mr. Salter, you'll have to tell me everything—without exception."

Crumbling under the intensity of her gaze, the reporter nodded exhaustedly. "Alright, Miss Scott…I'll tell you what I can. I'm not sure you'll believe any of it, but what I'm about to say is God's honest truth."

She smiled mischievously and retook her seat. "Sherry?" she asked, pouring herself a large measure. He nodded reluctantly and took the proffered glass. His was only half as full as hers as she clinked their glasses and downed hers in one go. "Please continue, Mr. Salter," she said expectantly.

He began to speak, "It's all a bit hazy really. You see, to my knowledge, I believe that I'm the sole witness to a heinous crime, a murder perpetrated long ago. And without my testimony, nobody will ever know what really happened."

Intrigued, she interjected, "Now we're actually getting somewhere. Please, don't skip any details, Mr. Salter. You must leave nothing out."

He nodded, his cheeks flushed. "Not only am I the

remaining witness, I am the sole survivor. You see, the fact that I'm able to relay this story to you at all is a miracle in itself. And before you ask about my state of mind and to be completely transparent; I'm not sure that any of this is real. You, me, this desk," he said, rapping it sharply with his knuckles. "I can't say for certain that any of it actually exists."

Velma frowned as he spoke; it wasn't what she'd expected. She waited patiently for him to continue, scrutinising him carefully. "I'm not quite sure I follow you, Mr. Salter. Would you care to elaborate a little?"

The reporter sighed, "Well it's true…So there it is, I've said it. Believe me, I know how it sounds. However, let me reassure you, Miss Scott, I'm not crazy! I appreciate the caution in your response. But I'm not finished, and you did say not to leave anything out."

Velma topped up her drink and waited for him to continue. He breathed in deeply as if he were about to make a confession to his priest. "If I were to tell you, that as a child, I was subjugated to unusual rituals and experiments. A litany of them. All designed to induce telepathic reactions to make contact with another plane of existence…How would you react? What would you say?"

The detective coughed uncertainly. This didn't sound like one of the usual stories that came through her door. More often they were related to cases of fraud and embezzlement or sometimes grounds for divorce. She wasn't sure how to proceed. "Well, Mr. Salter, I'm in uncharted waters here. Philosophical or paranormal debate isn't really my specialty. I try to leave that to the experts."

The reporter laughed uneasily at her quip, "What experts?"

She shrugged, "You know priests, philosophers, mediums, necromancers, God…that sort of grouping."

The smile fell from his face and was replaced by a grimace. "Unfortunately, Miss Scott, it's all true. And many of your so-called experts were involved."

Velma leant back in her chair and closed her eyes pensively. "Can you prove any of what you're telling me, Mr. Salter? Do you have any evidence to support your claims?"

The reporter nodded slowly, "I have some, yes."

Surprised at his response, Velma reached into her desk drawer and pulled out a small clay pipe. "You mentioned that you were the sole witness to a crime?" She reminded him as she prised open the lid of a square tin on her desk and stuffed the pipe loosely with tobacco. Eyeballing him throughout the process, she took her time, studying him thoroughly.

The reporter nodded nervously as the detective struck a match and drew fiercely on the pipe as she lit it. The stench made the reporter cough, long before the smoke even reached him. Apprehensively he replied, "I was a witness to a murder, the drowning of a child. I know how it all sounds Miss Scott, you haven't changed your mind have you? You will still take my case?"

Velma hesitated before replying, "If it wasn't for your references and the small advance I've already accepted on your behalf from your editor, I'd have sent you packing. However, I've known your editor a long time, and he assured me that you are a trustworthy fellow. So even though your story sounds incredible, impossible even; I will endeavour to investigate your claims, no matter how odd they may sound."

The reporter sighed with relief and warmly shook her hand as he stood up. "I'll bring my research over tomorrow. You can review it and ask me anything you like. Shall we say around seven p.m.?"

She rested her pipe in the brass ashtray on her desk. Thick smoke wafted around her as she replied, "Very well, Mr. Salter. We'll talk again tomorrow evening." She opened the office door for her new client and watched as her assistant escorted him out.

Impatiently she waited for her to return. "Janice?" she called, "I'll need you to do some digging for me in the morning. Check the usual sources and get me a full background report. Tomorrow, I want you to find out all you can about our new client, Mr. Salter. He'll be back here around seven p.m. So, before then, alright my dear?" Pursing her lips as she decided what to record, Janice jotted down a note in her diary. "He looked distraught. What kind of trouble is he in exactly?"

The detective shook her head uncertainly. "I'm not sure yet, Janice. That's part of the thrill. I'm hoping that we'll learn more tomorrow."

THREE

Velma Scott stared incredulously at the overflowing crates of papers strewn across her desk. Her gaze rose to meet the expectant face of the reporter, Douglas Salter. "You seem to have gathered quite a lot of information. A lot more than I would have imagined…"

The journalist smiled tightly, "You said you wanted to see all the evidence I've collected. Well, this is everything I've managed to find," he said, spreading out his arms expansively.

The detective nodded regretfully, "Yes, I did say that, didn't I? Tell me, Mr. Salter, has anything else happened since we met yesterday? Have there been further attempts on your life?"

The reporter shook his head with relief. "Not yet. At least nothing so far, Miss Scott."

"Good, good…" Velma murmured distractedly as she began to root through crates of papers and reports. She pulled out a file marked: *Secret, UK eyes only* and opened it inquisitively. Arching her eyebrows she asked, "How on

earth did you manage to get hold of something like this?"
The journalist shrugged, noncommittally.

"In 1956, researchers from a coastal research centre
conducted a study aboard a submerged Soviet submarine,"
Velma read aloud. "A Soviet scientist (Dr. Pavel Naumov)
conducted an animal biocommunication study. During the
course of the experiment, a rabbit that had recently given
birth had electrodes implanted into her brain. At the same
time, technicians aboard a submerged submarine began to
execute her litter, at predesignated times." As she read on,
the reporter rubbed his eyes wearily.

"Each occurrence of death aboard the submarine
was noted and recorded. Simultaneous readings were taken
at the land-based research lab. They checked the mother's
brain activity at the predesignated times of death of her
litter. In each individual case of death, detectable and
recordable reactions were made in the mother's brain."

Nodding sadly the reporter replied, "The complete
set of results from the experiment remain out of reach.
They're locked behind the Iron Curtain."

"How the devil did you get hold of this?" Velma
asked. "This report details secret Soviet experiments. And
it's classified as UK eyes only?"

"It's my job," Douglas replied simply. "I've made
a few useful contacts down the years, much like your own
profession, I imagine, Miss Scott?"

The detective nodded warily, closed the file, and
placed it to one side. "So how exactly does this report tie in
with your claims, Mr. Salter?"

Douglas smiled weakly, "I think I mentioned
yesterday that as a child, I was a test subject. That a series

of experiments and rituals were conducted on me and other children."

"Didn't your parents have something to say about it?" asked Velma curiously.

Douglas shook his head, "No, I was raised in an orphanage. I never knew my parents."

"Oh, I see, forgive me for prying," replied Velma quietly. "Please go on, Mr. Salter. I'm curious as to how you think this report supports your alleged claims?"

"It's proof of telepathy," he replied determinedly. "The experiment shows that there's a measurable mental link between a mother and her children."

Intrigued despite her reservations, Velma looked from the file to the reporter. She studied his face closely, "But the experiment described here looked at the relationship between a doe and her litter? Forgive me for saying this, but you don't appear to be a rabbit. And you said yourself, you never knew your mother. I really don't see the connection."

The reporter's face turned crimson, "I'm trying to show you that telepathy actually exists. That it's measurable, scientifically. That it's real!"

Velma bit her lip and pulled another file from the crate. Casually, she flicked through it. "Mr. Salter, do you mind if I call you Douglas?"

He shook his head, "No, that's fine Miss Scott."

She peered at him over her half-moon spectacles, "You know, there's quite a lot to go through here. This could take a while. Why don't we pop out for some dinner? You look like you could use a drink or two. My local's just up the road and you can tell me more whilst we eat."

Douglas grinned, "I like the sound of that, first drink's on me."

The detective slipped on her shoes and buttoned up a severe-looking overcoat. "You're the one that's paying my dear. I'm afraid that any expenses accrued are entirely down to you."

The reporter shoved his hands into his pockets and smiled awkwardly as she hooked her arm through his. "Janice!" Velma bellowed as they headed towards the office door.

Her assistant's head popped through the doorway, "I've told you before Miss Scott," she scolded. "You don't have to shout, I can hear you perfectly well."

The detective grinned at her assistant. "Janice, this nice young man has kindly offered to take me out for dinner. Why don't you close up early and go home?"

"Really?" harrumphed Janice, choosing to ignore the bright hue of the reporter's cheeks. "And drinks as well I suppose?" Velma nodded delightedly. The detective's assistant clicked her tongue with irritation. "You watch out for her after a couple of drinks, Mr. Salter," she advised the reporter. "She has a horrible tendency to find trouble."

Chuckling, Velma replied, "I think you've got that the wrong way around, Janice. I don't go looking for trouble, but somehow, it tends to find me."

The reporter looked uncertainly from the petite fiery redhead to the detective. "Perhaps you could join us?" he suggested, feeling suddenly apprehensive at the thought of spending an evening alone with Velma Scott.

"I think that's a splendid idea, Douglas," cooed the detective, winking at her secretary. "Janice, go and grab your coat!"

They hurried him down the stairs and into the street below. Interlinking their arms on either side of him, the detective and her assistant marched the reporter to the pub at the far end of the street. "This is really very kind of you, Mr. Salter," enthused the detective as they neared their ominously named destination: *The Devil's Punchbowl.*

"It's quite all right," he murmured distractedly, tearing his gaze away from Janice's bewitching green eyes. "If you'll find a table, I'll go and order some drinks from the bar."

Velma grinned, "That sounds like an excellent suggestion, my dear. I'll have a large whisky and soda and a G&T for Janice. Ask them to bring over a menu as well, will you?"

Douglas nodded and held open the pub door for the detective and her assistant. *Sorry,* Janice mouthed to him as she followed after her employer. The reporter sighed resignedly, checked his wallet, and headed to the bar. *I'm going to need more than a few drinks to get through this,* he decided.

FOUR

Several hours later, in a secret central London government laboratory, a cleaner mopping the floor came across the still and rigid form of a rabbit. It lay unmoving on its side, resting on an examination table. He prodded it gingerly with the end of his mop and rolled it over to inspect it. After checking for signs of disease and noting how well-fed it looked, he decided to take it home for his wife to cook for dinner.

***

"Where the heck did you get this rabbit from?" asked the cleaners' wife, as her husband let out a deep sigh of contentment, rubbing a chubby hand on his round stomach, "I've not seen one in the butcher for quite a while. Was it expensive? Did it cost an arm and a leg? You know we have to watch the pennies this month," she continued.

With rationing still in place, it had been a while since either of them had eaten fresh meat, and he felt happy and content for the first time in what seemed like an age. "That was a lovely spot of dinner, Minnie," he called out to his wife, ignoring her questions. The cleaner downed a glass of homebrew and began to absently probe his mouth with one of his wife's knitting needles. He picked around haphazardly, attempting to remove the last vestiges of meat from his teeth.

The rattle of pots and pans emanated from the kitchenette as his wife cleared up. He swaggered into the kitchen, humming enthusiastically. "Let's go to bed, woman," he suggested, grabbing her eagerly around the waist and spinning her around.

"Alfie, you're drunk!" she scalded, pushing him away and wagging her finger at him.

He roared with laughter, "I'm only drunk for you, my love." He chuckled and began chasing her around their small flat. Laughing, she kicked open the bedroom door, tugging on his arm. "You've promises to keep," she teased, giggling as they fell onto the bed together.

FIVE

A desperately hungover research assistant got into his lab the following morning. His birthday celebrations had continued long into the night, and he definitely felt worse for wear. Today, he was late and appeared even more unkempt than was usual. His hair was scraggly, and his creased shirt belied the fact that he lived life as a bachelor.

There was nothing remarkable about the fact that he was late. His clocking in card undoubtedly revealed that very fact. The research assistant was late for work more often than he arrived on time. Still, today he was later than was normal, even for him.

He slumped down at his bench, nursing his pounding head in his hands. It took three strong black coffees and a further hour before he realised that something was wrong. Very wrong.

Worriedly, he began to pace up and down his lab. His face took on a sickly green hue as he checked and rechecked where his research project should have been.

Miserably, he picked up the phone, ready to report it to his superiors. He didn't realise it, but the fact remained that even if he'd managed to arrive on time, he would have been too late. His experiment had gone missing, long before he was due back in the lab that morning.

The consequences of losing such a valued resource filled him with trepidation. He decided that there was only one course of action; to absolve himself of any blame. Hurriedly, he hung up the phone and instead recorded the missing rabbit as having passed away. *Probably heartbroken*, he reasoned, as he attributed its death to natural causes in the laboratory logbook. *Another loyal servant of Her Majesty's government*, he mused darkly.

***

A previous few hours…

The rabbit, Beatrice, had been understandably furious before her death. Induced into a semi-hypnagogic state as part of an ongoing experiment, she'd remained conscious and yet separated from her body for over forty-eight hours. *A new laboratory record!*

Beatrice had realised early on that her principal carer, the research assistant, had failed to lock her away for the night. On top of that, another imbecile of a human had removed her from the laboratory she called home.

She guessed that her carer, the researcher, would have been delighted if he'd been aware of the new milestone they'd achieved together. But now, he'd never know.

The circumstances surrounding her untimely death certainly exacerbated the situation. An incorporeal Beatrice watched with horror, as her body was mutilated by the cleaner's wife. Wincing as the knife cut repeatedly into her flesh, she swore vengeance. Not just for the violence inflicted on her, but on her dearly departed, darling children as well.

The actions of these humans within and outside of the research facility had resulted in her soon-to-be-untimely demise and that of her litter. Her heartbeat gradually slowed as she watched the cleaner's wife disembowel her body. Beatrice, the rabbit, was apoplectic. Furiously, she began to demand justice from the dead.

Her little body clung desperately to life, as she wrestled with the horror befalling her. With a dull thud, the kitchen knife swung down hard and lopped off her head. Finally detached from her mortal coil, her mind roamed free. Yet a single thought stayed with her, anchoring Beatrice somewhere between the world and the afterlife. The final thought that formed coherently in her mind was: *I want revenge!*

SIX

William Russell was the unfortunate research assistant's immediate superior. He was also the government's Chief Scientist and Science Advisor. His own superior, the Defence Chief, Harold Cage, wasn't a happy man. He'd made that perfectly clear during the course of their mid-morning meeting.

Russell wasn't the kind of man who enjoyed being berated, especially by someone he deemed to be both paranoid and, more than likely, a deranged sociopath. On top of that, he'd received the dressing down in front of the Minister. The whole experience had left him feeling depressed and irritable.

As a result, he wasn't in the best of moods either. And Russell was determined to make that point very clear to the slovenly, bumbling figure sat opposite him. *Why shouldn't he feel as miserable as I do?* Sternly, he stared down the end of his horn-rimmed spectacles and glared. The research assistant shuddered as his superior followed up his malicious look with a loud crack of his knuckles. "Let's start again shall we? What exactly happened to the rabbit?"

Blinking rapidly as he ran through a raft of scenarios in his mind, the research assistant took a deep breath before answering, "I entered her death into the logbook."

Russell nodded irritably, "Yes, I'm aware of what you recorded. But what were the exact circumstances?"

Flailing for a reply, the research assistant paled. "Actually, I'm not too sure," he stammered.

Impatiently, Russell ground his teeth, he was in no mood for this fellow's prevarication. "Well, I'm not sure I can make my question any clearer. Let me ask you once more. And for your own sake, let's hope you can provide an adequate answer. What did the rabbit die from and where is its corpse now?"

The research assistant stared helplessly out of the window, trying to avoid the gaze of his interrogator. He gulped down the bile that was accruing at the back of his throat and racked his hungover brain for a reply. In an already fragile state, his mind refused to work quickly enough. "I…erm…" he mumbled.

His superior's glare took on a fresh intensity as the research assistant struggled to find any meaningful words. "Well? What's your answer?" snapped Russell. "Come on, I haven't got all day—speak up man!"

Squirming in his chair, the research assistant eventually shook his head. Unable to answer the question satisfactorily, he meekly whispered, "I really don't know, sir."

"What do you mean, 'you don't know'?" Russell countered.

"She was already missing," the man finally confessed with a sob. "I don't know what happened to her. I arrived at the lab this morning and Beatrice was gone. I've no idea how it happened. I've looked everywhere, I'm so sorry."

"Sorry?" fumed his superior. He stood abruptly from behind his desk and stomped towards the unfortunate research assistant. "Do you think sorry will disguise the fact that you've managed to lose a very important and costly experiment? Don't you realise the importance of that research project? It was vital to our national interest, to the very Defence of the realm. To say nothing about the expense and time involved. That blasted experiment has already taken three years and cost us nearly a million pounds."

Sinking deeper into his chair, the research assistant quivered at the verbal onslaught. "It's not my fault," he wailed. "You can't blame me! I promise you that I had nothing to do with her disappearance."

"Well, exactly whose fault is it?" snapped Russell. "Who should I be blaming? I know it's not my fault, and yet, I'm the one who had to report it. I'm the one that had to inform the Minister that we'd squandered a million-pound project. Can you even conceive of the response I received? And then to make matters worse, you're trying to cover it up!"

Tears began to roll down the research assistant's plump cheeks. "Sir," he pleaded desperately. "I can't be held solely responsible for her disappearance. I had absolutely nothing to do with it."

Russell sniffed the air between them suspiciously,

"Your pathetic attempts at an explanation really do stink." The research assistant nodded forlornly, he'd already realised that this wasn't going to end well. *I suppose I could always go back to teaching,* he speculated.

His superior returned to his seat and depressed a hidden button beneath his desk. Moments later, the doors to his oak-panelled office flew open. The research assistant bleated as two burly figures escorted him roughly out of his chair and towards the door. "Please," he whined, "I really don't know anything else."

Russell replied sharply, "How can I believe anything you say when you've already tried to deceive me? I'm afraid that interrogation is the only avenue left open to us. We must ensure that you haven't sabotaged the project on purpose. That you're not a Soviet informer!"

"Please, sir!" the research assistant cried out as the two burly figures dragged him out of the office, his shoes scuffing along the floor.

Sighing resignedly, Russell picked up the telephone. "Yes, of course, it's urgent," he snapped. "Put me through to the Minister's office at once." Impatiently, he drummed his fingers on the desk as he waited for his call to be transferred. *There was going to be hell to pay. And he wasn't going to bear the brunt of it alone. Life belongs to those who can pay for it.*

SEVEN

Douglas Salter frowned and hung up the telephone. It was the third call he'd received in as many hours that day. He dabbed at his forehead with his handkerchief and reached inside his desk drawer for a bottle of scotch he kept there for emergencies. It was also the third time he'd answered the phone, only to be met by a long, suffocating silence.

Feeling unnerved, he glanced over at his editor's empty desk as he poured himself a drink. Unsure what to do, he toyed with the idea of phoning Velma's office. He sighed loudly and then shook his head. *It's probably just a wrong number*, he thought, doing his best to reassure himself.

***

By the end of the day, Douglas had received six more sinister phone calls. And each time he'd answered, he was met with the same ominous wall of silence. By this point, he'd resolved that it was more than just a wrong number. With a sense of foreboding, he'd called the detective's office and tried to explain what had happened.

"Do you want me to come and meet you after work?" offered the detective.

Feeling both unnerved and uncertain, Douglas declined her offer. He wasn't sure how much help she could offer in a physical encounter. Instead, he'd found himself agreeing to an unorthodox suggestion from the detective's assistant, Janice. He couldn't say why, but he'd found her an impossible person to say no to.

***

The séance began early, deep in the East End of London. Velma glanced over at her assistant in the seat opposite and grinned. Janice frowned at her employer and loosened her grip on the neighbouring hand holding hers. She held her finger sternly to her lips; this wasn't the time or place for one of the detective's quips.

Douglas eagerly sought out Janice's hand again and gently but firmly squeezed it as the séance leader began the session. "Please close your eyes and focus, ladies and gentlemen. Let me remind you that we must have absolute quiet."

Velma stifled a yawn and opened one eye to check if anyone had noticed. Janice was glaring at her furiously from across the lace, covered dining table. The detective hurriedly shut her eyes and tried to focus on the voice of the séance leader. "Is there anybody there? Do you wish to make contact with us?" Huddled around the dining table, in the blacked out sitting room, the group waited intently for a reply.

Expectantly, in a mantra-like fashion, the séance leader repeated her words. "Is there anybody there? Do you wish to make contact with us?" Patiently, the group waited, but aside from the sound of their own breathing, the room remained ominously quiet.

Velma really wasn't sure if she was surprised or not. In her experience, these things were often a bit hit-and-miss. Nevertheless, her assistant, Janice, was convinced of the miraculous and mysterious powers of Mrs. Gladstone—the séance leader.

Despite her scoffing, Velma had found that on occasion, these sessions had proved surprisingly helpful during her previous investigations. That was why she'd agreed to Janice's suggestion and why they were there; despite the obvious misgivings of her client, Douglas Salter.

Velma glanced doubtfully at the assembled faces. Mrs. Gladstone, Janice, Douglas, Mrs. Wellington (a regular visitor to these sessions), and Mr. Bruce (The landlord of her local pub – where the séance was being held). They'd all lost someone, and each hoped for a sign that everything was all right on the other side.

The detective glanced at her watch, much to the chagrin of Mrs. Gladstone, who gripped her hand even more tightly. "Focus!" she hissed through gritted teeth. Velma smiled apologetically and closed her eyes. Mrs. Gladstone suddenly announced, "Yes! I'm sensing a presence." The group held their breaths expectantly. "I'm detecting a very unusual presence," she muttered as her eyeballs rolled back into their sockets and her breathing grew shallow. "Does anyone here know a Beatrice?"

With their eyes tightly shut, each of the participants shook their heads. "She's coming through again," the séance leader murmured excitedly. "Yes—it's definitely a Beatrice. Mr. Salter, I do believe that she wishes to commune with you."

Douglas felt Janice's fingertips softly stroking his hand. He fought the urge to open his eyes, "I'm sorry Mrs. Gladstone…but I really don't recall anyone of that name." The séance leader tilted her head to one side as if listening to a voice whispering into her ear. "Well, she definitely wants to talk with you. She's coming through very strongly now."

Determined to prove to Douglas and her employer that these things really were beneficial, Janice asked excitedly, "What's she saying, Mrs. Gladstone?"

The séance leader nodded her head as she listened. In a trance-like state she murmured, "Mr. Salter, she says that you both have a shared experience. She's saying that she was the subject of a horrendous experiment. And that you underwent a similar experience in your youth?"

Douglas Salter paled at Mrs. Gladstone's words. *This is impossible*, he thought to himself. *The detective must have said something*. His hands became sweaty, and he fought the urge to break contact and wipe them down his trousers.

"She knows that you doubt the sincerity of her words. But she says that she's going to help you track down the culprits. Beatrice is demanding justice for you, for her, and for her children. She wants revenge!"

Douglas opened his eyes and stared hard at the séance leader. "What kind of sick parlour trick is this?" His focus fell on those around the table, and each of them kept their eyes firmly shut. He suddenly felt very foolish and very angry. They were obviously taking advantage of him. Douglas grimaced and shook his hand free from Janice's clasp. "What did you tell her?" he growled accusingly. "What kind of bloody con-trick is this? I was told that you were a professional, Miss Scott."

His words and sense of fury broke the spell. Blinking, the assembled group opened their eyes and stared wonderingly at Douglas Salter. "Well?" he demanded, folding his arms expectantly. "What have you got to say for yourself?"

Mrs. Gladstone groaned as her body trembled from exertion, she groaned again as she tried to wrestle free from the vision. Finally, she opened her eyes, "This is no trick, Mr. Salter. That is simply what I was told by the spirit who made contact—Beatrice. I can assure you that neither Janice nor Velma have told me anything about you."

"Poppycock," he replied brusquely, standing up. "This is obviously a twisted trick of some kind, at my expense no doubt," he muttered, looking witheringly from Velma to Janice.

"Please sit down, Douglas," implored Janice. "Mrs. Gladstone has a real gift. That's how this works. I know it can seem…a little odd…but she's the real thing!"

He shook his head angrily, "That's enough, Janice. After this debacle, I'll no longer be requiring your so-called expertise. Douglas shot Velma a venomous look, "I'll deal with this matter on my own." He stormed out of the room, slamming the door shut behind him with such force that the pictures on the walls shook.

"I'm so sorry, Mrs. Gladstone," apologised Janice.

"I know you were just trying to help."

The séance leader patted Janice's hand lightly, "It's alright my dear. Some people can find this a very unsettling experience. It's not your fault."

Velma stood up and pulled on her overcoat, "I'll try and catch him up, Janice. Why don't you head back to the office?"

Nodding as she stifled back tears, Janice pecked Mrs. Gladstone on the cheek. "I'm so sorry," she apologised again, before hurrying out of the room.

Velma regarded Mrs. Gladstone pensively, *Perhaps there really is something to all this.* She thanked and paid the séance leader before hurrying downstairs and searching the bar, but Douglas Salter was nowhere to be found.

EIGHT

arold Cage, the head of the Defence Intelligence staff, glowered at the Minister as he grudgingly relayed the contents of William Russell's telephone conversation. Despite his reservations, the Minister couldn't tear his eyes away from the purple hue that gripped the Defence Chief's face as he spoke.

"What does he mean he's lost it? How on Earth do you lose a top secret, million-pound project from within a secure location?"

The Minister shrugged helplessly. He was more than a little intimidated by the man, who appeared uninvited in his office on a regular basis. Cautiously he suggested, "Perhaps it's still there? It could have simply escaped and be wandering the corridors somewhere."

"Has he bothered to check?" demanded the Defence Chief. The Minister, already regretting his decision to volunteer a suggestion, shrugged again. "Tell him I'm on way over," growled Cage. The Minister's hand moved towards the Bakelite telephone perched on his oak top desk. "Stop!" ordered the Defence Chief suddenly, banging his fist down. "I'll pay him an unannounced visit. That'll be much more satisfying."

Nodding, the Minister hurriedly withdrew his hand and breathed a sigh of relief as Cage stomped out of his office. *What a bloody mess*, he mused, pouring himself a large scotch. Sipping at it tentatively, he opened the file on his desk and reread the report that the Defence Chief had prepared for him.

"Incredible," he muttered disbelievingly. He knew from his own time during the war how paranoid the intelligence staff could be, and none more so than their Chief, Harold Cage.

The Minister swirled the ice around in his glass. *Cage enjoys wrapping himself in a cloak of paranoia*, he thought to himself. *Maybe it makes him feel in control of things*. He glanced over the report's summary and finished off his drink. The Minister wasn't sure what he thought after reading through the report, but even still, it sounded remarkable.

He would of course have to inform the Prime Minister of this failure. How to tell him without Cage hearing of it would be the tricky part, he mused. The Defence Chief wouldn't be happy, he was certain of that. And neither would the Prime Minister, once he'd learnt of what had happened.

Sighing heavily, the Minister poured himself another large whisky and sank back into his worn leather chair. He glanced worriedly at his door. *If even a portion of what he'd read was true…*he shivered at the thought and snapped the file shut.

NINE

Gloomily, Douglas nursed a fourth double scotch in his hand. After the third, his anger had begun to abate, and a reassuring sense of calm had descended. He swilled the honey-coloured nectar about in the glass and caught sight of his reflection in the mirror behind the bar. His face looked drawn with heavy, dark rings circling his eyes.

Even now, the clammy sensation he'd experienced during the séance had refused to wipe from his hands. Perched uncomfortably on a bar stool in a pub opposite Southgate tube station, he wondered what to do.

"Douglas Salter?" interrupted a baritone voice, shattering his mood of quiet introspection.

He caught a glimpse of a face in the bar mirror before he turned to face him. "Yes, that's me," he sighed despondently. "Who wants to know?"

"I've been trying to contact you for days," complained the figure, still staring at him with annoyance. "Don't you bother to check your messages?"

Irritated by his tone, Douglas sized the man up. He was squat and broad-shouldered with tight black curls and a menacing look. Douglas scowled, "I'm in no mood for games. What do you want?"

The man smiled guardedly, "I just wanted to talk with you, that's all."

Douglas shook his head, he felt emboldened by the drink. "Well, I've had a hell of a day pal. And to be honest, I really don't want to talk to anyone right now. Why don't you call me tomorrow?"

Any pretence of friendliness vanished from the man's countenance. "Now listen here," he began, jabbing his finger sharply into Douglas's chest. "There's no need to take that kind of attitude. I'm just here to pass on a simple message."

Douglas brushed the man's hand away irritably and rose unsteadily from the barstool. "I'm not interested in you or your message. Just clear off, will you?"

Leering, the man stepped onto Douglas's toes, his weight holding him in position. "I've a warning for you, Salter. Stop digging into matters that don't concern you, otherwise, you'll pay the price."

Douglas giggled drunkenly, "What the hell are you talking about? I'm not digging into anything?" The squat figure frowned; *this wasn't how he'd expected the conversation to go.* "Are you a workman? Are you doing the digging?" asked Douglas uncomprehendingly.

The man's temper flared. He growled, "Are you deliberately misunderstanding what I'm telling you?"

Douglas shook his head in bafflement. "I've genuinely no idea what you're talking about. You're not making any sense. Are you sure you're talking with the right person?"

At this point, the man was beginning to wonder that himself. He stepped off the reporter's toes and stared at him quizzically. "You are the reporter, Douglas Salter?" Douglas shrugged, "Who can say for sure? You know earlier on today," he slurred, "I was communing with a spirit. And I don't mean this one!" he giggled, shoving his glass under the man's nose.

The squat figure frowned, *This idiot was too drunk to understand a word he was saying, let alone understand the message he was trying to convey.* "Look, I'll make this easy for you," he hissed. Douglas didn't see the fist until it was too late. The man struck him with a glancing blow to the stomach.

The reporter groaned and doubled over. Coughing, he held onto the bar for support and valiantly tried not to vomit. Unfortunately, or fortunately, depending on your perspective, he couldn't quite stop himself. The altercation didn't stir pub regulars as they were accustomed to sporadic brawls erupting out of nowhere.

Bile began to flow from his mouth and nose. Then it gushed out unrepentantly in a torrent over the other man's shoes. Wiping his mouth, Douglas regained his composure slightly and drew himself upright. He heaved again suddenly and spewed another vomit-driven projectile into his assailant's face. Speechless, a look of pure venom crossed the squat figure's features as he tried to wipe himself down. Douglas hooted with laughter, "Well, that about serves you right doesn't it!"

The man was about to swing again when an umbrella handle hooked itself around his arm. It twisted this way and that, spinning the man's arm around like a children's toy. He turned to see who'd dared to intervene. The umbrella handle suddenly hooked around his throat and slammed his head against the corner of the bar. His body slumped and fell limp and unconscious to the floor.

"Miss Scott!" Douglas cried happily. "You certainly have a remarkable sense of timing. How on earth did you find me? I feared things were about to get a little awkward."

She stepped over the prostrate figure on the floor. "I called your editor and he suggested a few places I might find you. Are you alright Douglas? You look a little worse for wear."

"Thanks for lending a hand, but I think I had it all under control." He nodded at her and waved a note at the barman, "I'm starting to sober up actually. What do you want?"

Velma shook her head, "I think you've had enough already Douglas. Let's go before your friend wakes up. You can buy me some fish and chips on the way home."

"My friend?" he replied uncertainly, stumbling against the body on the floor. "Ah yes, you mean this chap. He was blathering on about all sorts of gibberish, you know?"

Velma nodded patiently, she felt relieved to have found her client. "Well, I suppose you're right, Miss Scott. Fish and chips would be lovely actually." Drunkenly, he grinned at her, "Best quit whilst I'm ahead, eh?"

She nodded patiently, and Douglas pocketed the pound note, whilst wiping spots of vomit on his shoes against the unconscious body on the floor. Velma linked her arm tightly through his to prop him up. "The fish and chips are on me Miss Scott, my treat!"

"Yes, dear," she replied, patting his arm reassuringly. "That's very considerate of you Douglas. Come on Mr. Salter, let's get you out of here before your friend wakes up."

TEN

The sudden and unexpected appearance of a belligerent Harold Cage caused William Russell to consider an alternative career. He'd long wondered if he should return to a simpler time and his former academic life. Oxford's dreaming spires beckoned him as he did his best to ignore the foul-mouthed tirade that was currently headed his way.

"And another thing…" the Defence Chief spat. "What kind of shambles are you bloody well running here? It's absolute chaos! And I'm being generous with that."

Russell sighed and knocked back another whisky, his third, of an already fraught day. "Please calm yourself, Mr. Cage. Interrogators have questioned the research assistant and found nothing untoward. It's just a simple case of bad luck, these things happen from time to time. We'll just have to start again."

"Start again?" spluttered the Defence Chief. "Three bloody years, we've spent on these experiments. Do

I need to remind you of the threat that this country faces? Do you think that our enemies are prepared to wait until we're ready before they start the next war?"

Shaking his head, Russell replied exasperatedly, "No, of course not. I'm fully aware of our tenuous position."

Cage harrumphed, clearly unimpressed by the response of the government's Chief Science Advisor. "Exactly how long will this mess delay our work on the psychic resonator?"

Russell sighed again. "It's hard to tell. Without the rabbit as our test subject, it'll delay the human trials. I'd say another year, maybe two."

"Two years?" spat Cage. "It'll be too bloody late by then. A third world war will have begun and ended. Why don't we just roll over now and save ourselves the bother?"

Russell nodded wearily as he waited for the other man's anger to subside. "Even if the rabbit were still alive, we'd still have to conduct at least a year's worth of human trials beforehand. We haven't even identified any potential candidates at this point."

"Well I have," growled Cage. "Whilst you've been twiddling your bloody thumbs, Russell, I've been getting my hands dirty. After much endeavour, I have identified two potential candidates. All of whom have displayed some promise in this area. I want to begin human trials as soon as possible."

"But we're nowhere near ready!" protested Russell, alarmed at what he was hearing.

"You will be ready," warned Cage. "The human

trials of the psychic resonator will begin next month. We must weaponise telepathic thought before our rivals do. It's the only thing that can save this country from being relegated to the second tier. We will not become a second-rate power on my watch."

"But…" Russell interrupted helplessly. He was silenced by the stern look on the Defence Chief's face and his raised finger.

"You have one month, Mr. Russell. Otherwise, you'll be joining your late research colleague at the bottom of Loch Lomond."

Russell gulped nervously, "My late colleague?"

The Defence Chief grinned nastily. He hovered in the doorway of the Chief Science Advisor's office and scowled in his direction. "Let me remind you, Mr. Russell, there's no room for failure. As your former research assistant has just found out for himself."

The office door slammed shut and Russell sank his head miserably into his hands. "A month?" he muttered, shaking his head, "it's impossible!"

ELEVEN

Douglas's head pounded when he woke. "Oh my god," he muttered as the room began to spin. Desperately, he closed his eyes to try to stem the movement, but it just made things worse. Groaning, he rolled over and landed with a thud on the floor. The reporter laid there unmoving, not daring to open his eyes. Stifling the urge to throw up, he waited, sensing that the room's motion was still in full flow.

A clatter outside forced him warily to open one eye and he took in the ceiling of an unfamiliar room. "Oh!" he exclaimed with surprise. Wondering where he was, Douglas licked his dry, cracked lips. He looked up at the sofa he'd fallen from, none the wiser as to his location. His throat felt parched and he licked his dry lips thirstily.

"Good morning, Douglas," exclaimed Velma Scott cheerily as she pushed open the door. A tray rattled noisily in her hand as she entered the room. The detective set it down with a clang on her desk, "Breakfast for two, my dear. Come on, get up and tuck in before it gets cold."

Douglas shuddered and shut his eyes again. "Where am I? What are you doing here?"

The detective chuckled, "You're on the floor of my office, my love. Looks like you took a fall during the night. Come on now, I've a business to run. Get up!"

Douglas staggered ungainly to his feet, he was still drunk. The smell of eggs wafted towards him, turning his stomach. He groaned and then realised he was standing there barelegged. His face turned scarlet. He was missing his trousers. "Oh Christ," he muttered.

Velma chuckled, "Nothing to worry about dear. Let me reassure you that at my age, I've seen it all before."

"We didn't?" he asked, aghast.

"A lady never reveals the truth about these things," she replied, grinning wickedly.

Douglas felt sick, even sicker than he had only five minutes previously. "Please tell me what happened?" he begged.

Ignoring his question, she simply replied, "Pop your trousers back on my dear, and come and eat something. I've squeezed some fresh orange juice. You'll probably need your strength after last night's escapades, and besides, they're full of vitamins."

Mortified, he did as he was told, not daring to look her in the eye. "I'm afraid that last night is a bit blurry. I'm very sorry but I really can't remember a thing."

"I'm not at all surprised," she replied, scooping off the top of her egg and dipping her toast into the yolk. "You'd drank a skinful."

He nodded forlornly, not daring to ask more as he took the seat opposite her. "So," she began breezily. "Do you still want me to work your case? It's quite all right if you want me to stop, but I'm afraid that your deposit is non-refundable at this point."

Douglas shuddered, as the memory of the séance forced itself back into his already pounding head. "I was annoyed at what happened at that bloody séance yesterday. Neither you nor Janice should have said anything. I told you about myself and my situation in confidence. I expected you to respect my privacy and to be discreet."

"Oh, I never break a confidence," replied Velma, tucking into her eggs with gusto. "Neither does Janice. You'll have to accept what happened yesterday at face value. I know it's difficult. I've had some problems accepting the truth of it myself. But you must admit, it's no stranger than the tale you've told me."

Douglas didn't respond, he was watching egg yolk dripping down the detective's chin. He looked away uncomfortably. "You're telling me that what happened yesterday at the séance was for real?"

She grinned at him, "Yes, I am Douglas. By the way, you should apologise to Janice. She was quite distraught after your little tantrum. And she won't like me saying this, but she was quite tearful after you stormed out."

Douglas nodded as he recalled his outburst. "I will Miss Scott. I really didn't mean to hurt her feelings."

Velma smiled warmly, "Good, it's settled then. Actions speak louder than words Douglas, besides; Janice will be pleased as punch. She's such a sensitive soul, you know?"

The reporter nodded regretfully and gulped down the glass of orange juice Velma passed over. "Right," she began, "to business. Do you still want me to continue my investigation?" The reporter's face turned pale as he watched Velma stick her tongue deep into the egg yolk lapping it up. He felt distinctly queasy and found himself unable to reply. Instead, he simply nodded.

The detective beamed at him, egg yolk smeared across her lips. "I think that's very sensible of you Douglas. Especially after your little adventure last night." Fighting the urge to vomit, he nodded again. "Do you recall your run-in with that rather rugged-looking fellow?"

Douglas strained to remember. Fleetingly, he caught a glimpse of a short, curly haired man. "I think he was trying to tell me something," he replied uncertainly.

"You vomited all over him," she announced pleasantly.

"Nasty-looking chap, I imagine he deserved it." The reporter nodded vaguely, he really couldn't remember.

"Anyway," Velma continued, "I imagine that you've got work you need to get to, Mr. Salter?"

He looked at her blankly, "Oh Christ, what time is it?"

"Just after six a.m.," Velma replied pleasantly. "I'm going to have a bit of a snooze, but you'll want to go home and change I imagine?" Douglas nodded as the room finally stopped spinning. "Why don't you pop by after work, shall we say around seven p.m.?"

Apprehensively, the reporter got up from his chair. He wasn't sure what to say. The best he could muster was, "Yes, later. Thanks for looking out for me last night, Miss Scott."

She grinned broadly, "It was my pleasure, Douglas,

all part of the service." She winked at him conspiratorially, "Don't worry—there's no extra charge for spending the night!" Douglas paled even more if it were possible and bolted out of her office. He hurried down the stairwell, accompanied by the sound of Velma Scott's raucous laughter.

TWELVE

The line clicked as the call was transferred. "Well, what have you got to report?" growled the Defence Chief abruptly over the telephone. "Did you manage to convey our message to that nosey reporter, Salter?"

The intelligence officer flinched at the Chief's words as he tenderly bathed his bruised eye socket with a wet towel. "I'm not sure he totally comprehended what I was trying to say, sir. To be honest, he appeared to be quite inebriated."

"It was a simple enough task, Beeton. All you had to do was to tell him to stop poking around in things that don't concern him. What exactly was the problem?"

Wincing as he removed the towel from his eye, he replied, "Someone intervened on his behalf, as I was trying to make myself clear."

"Who intervened?" snapped Cage, immediately suspicious. "Please don't tell me that you were prevented from delivering a simple message." The curly-haired figure muttered something incomprehensible down the line. "I didn't catch that. Speak up, man," growled Cage irritably.

"Yes, sir, I said a woman intervened."

The Defence Chief fought the urge to laugh as the intelligence officer told him of what had transpired. "Tell me about this woman Beeton, who was she? Did you recognise her? Do you think it likely that she was a Soviet operative?"

"I really don't think so, sir," the intelligence officer replied sheepishly. "She seemed a little old for that kind of thing."

Cage raised his eyes exasperatedly towards the ceiling of his office. "Are you trying to tell me that one of Her Majesty's top intelligence officers was assaulted by a pensioner?"

There was an uncomfortable pause before the intelligence officer eventually replied, "I'm sorry, sir." The line remained deathly silent as Beeton waited on a response from his superior.

"So, you've failed to deliver a simple message?" he heard his boss's voice in a whisper, barely audibly. The intelligence officer nodded uncomfortably, not daring to answer. Cage sighed exasperatedly. "If I wasn't short of qualified staff, I'd have you removed from your post. Sadly, I can't afford to do that right now. So, I'm prepared to give you one final chance, Beeton. Just deliver the bloody message—is that understood?"

"Yes, sir," the intelligence officer replied meekly, anxious for the call to end.

"Very well, I'll leave it in your hands, for now. What about the targets I've tasked you with identifying?

Have you managed to track them down yet? Do you have any positive news to report at all?"

"I'm meeting with the first one, Mrs. Gladstone, later today. I've booked myself on to one of her séances and will pass on your request. The other target is proving rather elusive to locate. I'm hoping to have more information later this evening."

"Don't fail me again, Beeton," warned Cage waspishly. "You know how I react when I'm disappointed."

The subordinate blanched at the Defence Chief's words. He well knew of Cage's reputation for disappearing people who'd displeased him. "I'm right on it, sir," he replied, with what he hoped sounded like total conviction.

"Very well—I'll expect a progress report tomorrow at the same time. Is that clear?"

"Yes, Mr. Cage," replied Beeton. "Actually, I'm about to speak with a contact of mine. I'm optimistic of a possible lead…" he began. The telephone line clicked dead as his boss hung up. Mopping his brow with the towel, the intelligence officer breathed a sigh of relief. Conversations with his superior always made him sweat profusely.

Beeton stared at his battered reflection in the mirror of his bathroom and promised himself that he'd make Douglas Salter pay for what he'd done. "Just you wait and see," he vowed.

THIRTEEN

Janice hung up the telephone, "Oh my God!" she gasped. Shaking, she stood up and hurried over to the adjoining door. "Miss Scott?" she banged urgently on the door with her fist. "Velma!"

The detective peered at her with concern as she opened it. "What is it, Janice? You look absolutely terrible."

"It's Mrs. Gladstone—she's been murdered!"

"Oh my," declared Velma, with surprise. "Are you sure?" Janice nodded, her eyes welling up. "You'd better come in, child," urged Velma. "Let me fix you a drink. In fact, let me fix us both one."

Janice nodded gratefully and slipped into the chair across from the detective's desk. "I can't believe it?" she stammered, shaking her head. "Why would anyone want to kill that sweet old lady? She's never hurt anyone."

Velma pressed a large sherry into her assistant's trembling hands. "Drink up, girl. It'll steady your nerves." She downed her own glass and poured a generous refill. "Do you know what happened? When and where the murder took place? Are there any suspects yet?"

Janice shook her head. "Mr. Bruce, the landlord, just called from the pub. He said the police had been round earlier this morning and that they'd been asking questions."

"What kind of questions?" asked Velma, looking quizzically at her assistant.

Sobbing softly, Janice shrugged helplessly. "I don't know what they were asking Miss Scott. I really can't believe it. It's just too awful for words."

The detective topped up Janice's glass. "Listen, I want you to call Douglas Salter. Ask him to meet me a little earlier today. Tell him not to visit any of his regular haunts after work. He should come straight here, do you understand? Don't let him argue, make sure he knows that his life may be in danger."

Janice nodded, "Do you think there's a link?" she asked worriedly.

"Perhaps," Velma replied, none too sure herself. "I'm going to pop over to Mrs. Gladstone's house to see what I can find out, alright?"

Blinking back tears, Janice smiled at her boss fondly. "Thanks, Miss Scott. I really don't know what I'd do without you."

Velma squeezed her assistant's shoulder fondly. "Things may be getting a little dangerous Janice. I don't want you to let in anyone that you don't already know. Is that clear?" she warned. Janice nodded her agreement as Velma pulled on her coat. "I'll see you later, my dear," the detective said, marching out of the office with her umbrella swinging from her arm.

Janice bolted the door shut as soon as the detective

left. Her hands still shaking, she helped herself to another sherry and took a long gulp. It warmed her stomach, but she was too on edge to really notice it. Cautiously, she looked out through the window into the street below. She couldn't see anything unusual or untoward. Janice let the blinds snap shut and she sagged down into the detective's chair, feeling utterly drained.

The clock on the wall in the office ticked loudly as she tried to process the news of Mrs. Gladstone's murder. Sniffling, Janice steadied her nerves and reached for the telephone across the desk. Attempting to compose herself beforehand, she picked up the receiver and dialled.

Janice had taken a liking to the detective's new client, the reporter, and she was already starting to worry about his safety. The pips on the phone did nothing to assuage her sense of dread as she waited. "I'd like to speak with Douglas Salter, please?" she requested as the operator finally answered. "Hurry please, it's urgent!"

FOURTEEN

The reporter paled as Janice informed him of the death of Mrs. Gladstone. "I'm so sorry," he eventually stammered down the telephone. "Are you all right?"

"I'm fine," sniffed Janice unconvincingly. "Miss Scott asked me to call you and to tell you to come over straight after work. She thinks that Mrs. Gladstone's murder could be connected to your case."

"I see," he responded, already feeling his nerves jangling. He reached into his desk drawer as she spoke and unscrewed the cap of a whisky bottle, which he kept in there for emergencies. *This is indeed a bloody emergency*, he told himself.

"She told me to warn you not to go anywhere you might visit regularly. It mightn't be safe." The reporter nodded as he listened, feeling on edge. "I'm really worried," Janice sobbed. "And I'm scared. I'm scared for you Douglas."

The reporter smiled despite himself. He wasn't

used to other people worrying about him. And he decided that he quite liked the feeling. "I should be out of here by six p.m. I'll come straight over afterwards Janice. Tell me, is Miss Scott there now?"

"No, she's not," wailed Janice miserably. Miss Scott's gone out to find out what she can about Mrs. Gladstone's murder. I'm all alone here."

"Don't worry about a thing Janice—just keep the doors locked. I'll be right over after work, I promise."

"Ok," she whimpered. "I'll talk to you later. Please be careful Douglas."

"You too, Janice," he replied softly.

***

Velma Scott marched up to the police officer posted outside Mrs. Gladstone's small terraced house. "Hello, Charlie," she began, "how's your old mum getting on?"

The bobby grinned, "Oh, she's keeping well, Miss Scott, and you?"

"I really can't complain," she replied, peering nosily over his shoulder towards the house. "So, I understand that poor Mrs. Gladstone has been murdered. Do you have any leads yet?"

He cracked his knuckles uneasily and replied, "You know I can't talk about that Miss Scott. The sergeant would have my hide."

She laughed good-naturedly, "I remember when I used to wipe your behind, Charlie. All those nights when your dear old mother was out scrubbing floors to put food

53

on the table. Where was your sergeant then?"

He looked away uncomfortably, "Please, Miss Scott," he begged. "I don't want to get in any trouble. I've only just passed my probation period."

"You won't get into any trouble," she promised. "I'm a professional investigator, Charlie. Whatever you tell me, I'll hold it in the strictest of confidences."

The policeman regarded her doubtfully. "Besides, you haven't always been a bobby in uniform have you Charlie? Do you remember when I saw you steal those sweets from Smith's shop on the corner when you were a boy?" Velma persevered. "Well, he's still wondering to this day who stole them."

Blushing with embarrassment, the policeman gave in. "Shush," he hissed awkwardly. "Please, don't say anything. I'm supposed to be seen as upholding the law."

She smiled kindly, "Charlie, I haven't said a word in 20 years, and I'm not about to start now. I just wanted you to know that I would never betray a promise."

"Alright, alright," he agreed hastily. "I'll tell you what I know." Velma grinned and nodded expectantly. "Poor Mrs. Gladstone's body was discovered early this morning by one of her neighbours. That was about six-thirty a.m. Normally they'd have a brew and a bit of a natter together at that time, and when she didn't show up, well…"

"Go on," pressed the detective.

He nodded hesitantly, "Mrs. Gladstone's body was discovered in the hallway of her home. She'd been stabbed several times and had been left to bleed to death."

"That's just terrible, it sounds awful," Velma

muttered. "So, do you have any leads yet?"

The policeman shook his head miserably, "No, nothing. Nobody saw anyone go in or out of her house last night or this morning. At this point, we're treating her death as unexplained."

Velma shook her head sadly. "She was a lovely woman, Mrs. Gladstone. I'm really going to miss her."

He nodded in agreement. "She used to read the tea leaves for my mum after my dad passed away. My mum will be distraught once she hears what's happened."

Velma nodded, "I think a lot of people will be upset when they hear about it. Do you mind if I take a quick look inside Charlie?"

The bobby shook his head, "I'm not sure that's a very good idea."

The detective patted his cheek lightly, "Give your mum my best, won't you?" She ignored his protests and eased past him, through the gate. Velma pushed lightly on the front door and let herself into the late Mrs. Gladstone's home.

There was a chalk outline on the floor and rouge bloodstains marked the lightly coloured rug. Velma carefully stepped over them, taking care not to disturb anything. She moved methodically from room to room, conducting a brisk search. Satisfied that she hadn't missed anything, she let herself out and closed the door firmly shut behind her. The policeman tipped his head and gave her a lopsided grin. "You didn't remove anything, did you?"

She shook her head, "No, of course not."

He nodded and said, "Take care of yourself, Miss Scott. Do you hear me? I'd hate to be standing outside your place like this one day."

She patted his cheek again fondly, "I'm sure I'll be quite safe with a good boy like you looking out for me." Velma rummaged inside her coat pocket and pressed a few jelly beans into the policeman's top pocket. "Just to keep you going," she said with a chuckle.

The policeman's cheeks flushed, and he stared after her as she ambled away. As he mused over how he was going to break the news of Mrs. Gladstone's death to his mother, he fumbled inside his pocket and stuffed a few of the sweets into his mouth.

Neither of them had been aware of the presence of the intelligence officer, Beeton, who suspiciously watched the proceedings with a great deal of interest. Ducking from behind the hedge where he'd been lurking, he surreptitiously began to trail the detective. He'd a score to settle with her and that blasted umbrella swinging from her arm like a broadsword.

FIFTEEN

Janice embraced Douglas tightly as he walked through the office door. "Oh Douglas, I'm so pleased you're safe, I've been worried sick and here alone all day."

Awkwardly, he unfurled her arms from around his neck. "Janice, I'm fine. There's no need to worry. Where's Miss Scott?"

She shook her head, "I've no idea. I haven't heard from her since this morning. I've been worrying over the pair of you."

"I'm sure she's fine Janice. She strikes me as a lady that can take care of herself." The detective's assistant nodded whilst she fussed over him. "Look, about the séance," he began. "I'm really very sorry. I shouldn't have said what I did. And I shouldn't have stormed out like that. Miss Scott set me right earlier this morning."

Janice nodded, tears welling up in her eyes. "It's my fault, Douglas. I shouldn't have made you go in the first place. If I had not done that, poor Mrs. Gladstone might still be alive. "

He shook his head, "It's not your fault Janice. If anyone's to blame, it's me. I'm the one that's embroiled you all in this. I feel terrible."

"Oh, don't say that," she gushed. "You weren't to know what'd happen. Listen, have you had a chance to think over what Mrs. Gladstone said? Who is Beatrice? Do you remember ever meeting anyone with that name?" Douglas shrugged helplessly, he was none the wiser as to the identity of the mysterious Beatrice.

The door suddenly barged open and the detective appeared in the doorway. She had a solemn look fixed on her face. "Ah, Mr. Salter, I'm glad you've arrived safe and sound. Janice, I appear to have picked up a tail. Can you find the camera for me?"

Janice looked at her with alarm, "A tail, are you sure?"

"Oh, yes," Velma replied. "Mr. Salter, would you mind looking through my office window, please? I think you might recognise him."

"Really?" he asked with surprise.

The detective nodded and replied, "Don't let him see you though. I doubt that he knows you're here." Douglas moved into the detective's office and peeled back the blinds. He glanced into the street below and waited. He was just about to turn around and inform her that he couldn't see anyone when a squat-looking figure gazed up at the window. Douglas let his fingers drop from the blinds. He didn't need a second look, the figure looked familiar; it was the man he'd run into at the pub. "When did he start following you?"

Velma beckoned him away from the window, "It

was earlier on this afternoon," she replied. "I'm not quite sure when I picked him up. I noticed his reflection in a shop window whilst I was browsing. That's why I've only just made it back to the office," she explained. As she shot a series of snaps with her camera, she called out, "I'm sorry you've been on your own all day, Janice. Your nerves must be frazzled."

Her assistant nodded, "I was starting to worry, especially after Mrs. Gladstone and all."

The detective smiled reassuringly at her. "Mr. Salter, why don't you walk Janice home? You can take the back door. I think she's had more than enough excitement for one day."

"What about you?" he replied. "I can't very well leave you here on your own, can I?"

Velma reached into her desk drawer and withdrew a heavy-looking club. "Oh, I'll be all right, Mr. Salter. I'm used to this kind of thing. Your friend down there is about to get the fright of his life."

"Please, let's just call the police," begged Janice, picking up the telephone.

"Put that down," scolded the detective sharply. "I'm looking for answers, and I think that brute down there might be able to provide some."

Douglas glanced at her worriedly. "Are you sure you don't want me to lend a hand? He seems rather menacing, don't you think?"

"I'll be quite all right my dear. Thank you for offering, Douglas, it's very thoughtful of you. But this is my neighbourhood, and we tend to police our own down here. I'll have all the help I need. I can assure you of that."

"Well, if you're sure?" he replied hesitantly, looking from her to Janice doubtfully.

The detective grinned at him. "Why don't you pop back once you've escorted Janice home? I'm sure all the excitement will have died down by then. Alright, my lovelies?"

Douglas wished away the crimson blush from his cheeks and prayed Janice hadn't noticed. He nodded and held open the door as Janice pulled on her coat. "I'll be back here shortly, Miss Scott. Please take care of yourself."

"I always do," replied the detective coolly. She bolted shut the door as they left via the fire exit and confidently sauntered down the stairwell.

SIXTEEN

Beeton glanced up at the detective's office window. *She'd had enough time to settle in*, he reckoned. Checking around beforehand and satisfied that he was alone, the intelligence officer began to jimmy the lock on the door. Focused on the task at hand, he didn't notice as a small gang approached him from behind. "What are you doing mate?" demanded the eldest-looking of the three.

Beeton quickly sized them up, taking in their biker's jackets and slicked back, Brylcreemed hair. "Bugger off," he replied over his shoulder, as they interrupted his work.

"That's Miss Scott's place. The light is on, mister, why don't you just ring the bell?"

Beeton ground his teeth as he shoved his pick back into his pocket. Irritably, he turned to face them and was surprised to find the detective amongst them. She smiled as she smacked a heavy-looking truncheon against her palm. "It's a perfectly reasonable question. Why haven't you just rung the bell?" she asked pleasantly.

The intelligence officer grimaced, this wasn't what he'd expected. He stared at her frostily as the youths swelled in number. "Miss Scott, is it? I was hoping we could talk?"

Velma nodded and took a step towards him. "Funny how these things work out," she replied. "I was hoping to have a word with you as well."

He nodded warily, "Perhaps we could speak inside?" he asked, gesturing up to her office with his thumb.

"I think right here will be fine," she replied easily, taking another step closer.

"What I have to say is of an extremely sensitive nature," muttered Beeton. "I really don't think that out in the street is a suitable place for discussions."

She smiled evenly, "I don't think you have to worry about that, my boys can be very discreet, can't you?"

"You know us, Miss Scott," replied the one nearest to her. He grinned nastily at Beeton as he unfurled a thick metal chain from his inside pocket. Beeton started to back away as the gang began to produce an array of homemade weapons.

"There's no need for violence," he muttered, looking over his shoulder for exits. He backed up against the door, all his exits blocked. "As I said, I just wanted to talk."

The detective chuckled, "So, why don't you start by telling me who you are?"

Rapidly assessing his diminishing odds, Beeton finally nodded. "My name's Frank. Frank Beeton. I wanted to talk to you about a case you're involved in. You're investigating the claims of a Douglas Salter. I've been asked to dissuade you by my employer."

"And who might that be?" Velma probed.

He hesitated, unsure of how much to divulge. "Let's just say that they're near the top of the tree," he replied.

"You're going to have to do a lot better than that, Frank," quipped the detective. "Who's your employer, and why don't they want me to investigate Mr. Salter's claims? Is your employer guilty of involvement?"

Beeton backed warily against the door as the gang started to close in around him. "My employer is very well connected, Miss Scott. They can make your life extremely difficult if they want to."

The detective frowned before replying, "I'm sure they can, Frank. However, I can make your life very difficult, right now."

The intelligence officer swore as the eldest-looking youth grinned at him. "Do you want us to beat it out of him, Miss Scott?"

"My employer works for the government," hissed Beeton. "If you lay a finger on me, you'll be in serious trouble. All of you!" Undeterred, the gang of youths began to laugh. The intelligence officer's cheeks turned crimson. "I'm warning the lot of you," he growled, pointing at them.

"Really, there's really no need for threats," the detective replied coolly. "You've passed along your message, and now I have a couple of questions for you. All you have to do is to answer them honestly, and you can go about your business. Doesn't that sound reasonable to you, Frank?"

Beeton carefully considered his position before answering. He had little room to manoeuvre. "Ask your bloody questions then," he snapped.

Smiling pleasantly, the detective repeated, "What is your employer's connection to Mr. Salter? And why do they want me to drop this investigation?"

"It's official government business, Miss Scott. I'm not privy as to the how and why. I've just been asked to relay a message."

Velma shook her head. "You're forgetting that I met you last night, Frank. You were assaulting Mr. Salter in the pub if you recall?"

"I was just trying to make myself clear," he argued. "Mr. Salter was more than a little drunk, and I was having trouble getting through to him."

"That's no reason to threaten his life," countered Velma sharply.

Beeton shook his head in confusion, "I did no such thing!"

"You didn't tail him after work and try to run him down?" quizzed the detective.

He shrugged helplessly, "I've no idea what you're talking about. I was just told to warn him off. Nothing more, I assure you."

Velma studied him closely, "Have you any idea who else would want to harm Mr. Salter? Are there any rival agencies involved in whatever it is you're doing?"
"I really can't help you," he replied sullenly.

"Very well Frank, I'll pass your message along to Mr. Salter. Please don't try to break into my office again. I might not be around to save you next time." Beeton nodded his agreement and edged away from the leering gang.

The detective watched him walk urgently away before grinning at her posse. "Thank you, boys, it was most kind of you to intervene."

"It was our pleasure Miss Scott," laughed the eldest looking. Anytime you need some muscle you just call us, alright?"

She chuckled and doled out handfuls of jelly beans into their eager hands. "I don't think there's a better cavalry anywhere."

***

Douglas nervously eyed the youthful-looking gang congregated outside Miss Scott's office as he pressed the buzzer and waited. One of them ambled towards him, chewing vigorously. "Is your name Salter?" he demanded. The boy was no more than sixteen, Douglas guessed.

The reporter nodded apprehensively, there were a lot of them loitering about and they vigilantly appeared to be eyeing him up. "Miss Scott said you're to meet her in the pub up the road. She said you'd know the one."

"She's all right then?" Douglas asked.

The youth nodded, and the reporter was about to thank him when he noted the boy's outstretched hand. He sighed with resignation and dropped some change into his hand. "Thanks, Mister," grinned the boy cheekily before scooting off towards his waiting friends.

Feeling relieved, the reporter turned and headed quickly to the pub. Habitually, he kept turning to look over his shoulder to check that no one was following. *Pull yourself together*, he told himself, as he saw the detective waving at him from the window of the pub. Velma Scott didn't appear to be overly concerned by little things like personal safety.

SEVENTEEN

The detective waved at him cheerfully as he entered through the door. "Mr. Salter! I'm glad to see you got my message. Is everything alright? Did you manage to get Janice home safely?"

"I did," he replied, sliding into the booth next to her. "Are you alright? What happened with the chap from the pub last night?"

She patted his hand lightly, "It's all taken care of Douglas. Don't you worry about that," she replied cryptically.

He regarded her expectantly, waiting for her to continue. Instead, she gazed forlornly at her empty glass until he took the hint. "Can I get you a refill?" he asked sheepishly.

Velma smiled at him gratefully, "That'd be wonderful Douglas, thank you. Do you remember my tipple?"

"Whisky and soda?" he checked. Velma grinned and patted his knee a little too fondly. Awkwardly, Douglas backed out of the narrow booth and retreated to the bar where he bought a round of doubles. He downed his in one swift motion and ordered a top-up before he headed back towards the expectant figure of Velma Scott.

"Well, did you find out who he was?" asked the reporter as he retook his seat. "Did you ask what he wanted?"

The detective idly swilled her drink about in the glass and peered intently at the reporter's face. "I did," she replied. "He's in the employ of the government, and he wants me to drop the investigation."

Douglas looked at her worriedly, "And are you going to?"

Velma sipped at her drink and let out a satisfied gasp. "That's not my style, Douglas. I've said I'll help you, and I will. But we're going to have to be even more careful. I don't think he's the only interested party."

The reporter's face fell as she spoke, "Oh," he murmured with worry.

"Cheer up, Douglas. If you look on the bright side, at least we can rule out the fact that your own government is trying to silence you."

He nodded without much enthusiasm. "Who does that leave then?"

The detective shrugged, "We've still to discover that aspect of the case. He said, he as in Frank, that he tried to warn you off last night, but you were too drunk to understand what he was saying."

It was the reporter's turn to shrug as he thought back to the previous evening. "Look, about last night..." he began hesitantly.

"Water under the bridge my dear," she chuckled. "Let's not talk about it right now. We've other things to discuss."

"We do?" asked Douglas.

"Certainly," she replied. "We need to draw up a list of possible suspects. If someone is out to get you, I want to know who and why."

The reporter nodded his agreement at the detective's logic and started to feel a little better about things as the alcohol began to take effect.

***

Beeton knocked back his lukewarm coffee and hurried across the road. He bustled into an empty phone box and relayed the news of Mrs. Gladstone's death to his boss. Beeton did his best to ignore the stream of profanities that came his way as Cage reacted with understandable displeasure at the news. "Well, that just leaves us with one more possibility. Have you had any success tracking him down yet?"

The intelligence officer mumbled a "no" and hurriedly moved on to more positive news as he confirmed the fact that he'd successfully relayed his boss's message to Salter and the detective.

"I'll give you another 24 hours to find the remaining target Beeton. Otherwise, I'll have you transferred. How does Northern Ireland sound to you?"

The intelligence officer fought the urge to argue his case. It wouldn't get him anywhere. "I won't rest until I've tracked him down, sir."

"Good man," growled Cage. "Now you sound motivated. Get on with it, man!"

"Yes, sir," replied Beeton miserably. He hung up and pushed aside the door of the phone box, just as the heavens opened. Cursing, he looked discontentedly up at the sky and hurried out into the rain.

EIGHTEEN

William Russell flinched as the rumble of thunder drew nearer. Tensely, he hung up the phone and began to massage his temples. He'd been fearful of storms ever since he was a child. Shivering as the memory rushed through his mind, Russell recalled sheltering underneath an oak tree just as a flash of lightning struck. He poured himself a drink to steady his nerves, as his secretary burst through the door. "Mr. Russell?"

"Yes?" he answered weakly.

"Sir, there's a problem."

"Yes?" he repeated, trying to disguise his already shaky demeanor.

"It's one of the cleaners, sir. He failed to appear for work today."

Russell sighed with relief, "I hardly think this qualifies under my purview, Sandra. Can't you call someone from the Estates Department? I'm sure somebody there can deal with it."

His secretary hesitated as she tried to gauge

his mood. She took a long, deep breath. She'd already determined that he wasn't going to like what she had to say, no matter how she said it. "Sir, you don't understand. Both the cleaner and his wife have been found dead. They may have been murdered."

"Dead?" repeated Russell, his pulse racing at the unexpected news, "Did you say they might have been murdered?"

"Yes, sir. When the cleaner didn't report for work last night, one of his colleagues went around checking on him this morning. They discovered his body, and that of his wife, dead in their home."

"I see," Russell replied, shuddering as another roll of thunder growled outside his window. "Well, I'm sorry to hear that Sandra. But what is it you want me to do about it?"

"There's a gentleman waiting to see you, sir, a policeman. I've asked him to wait, but he's very insistent."

"Is he outside now?" asked Russell, feeling his collar tightening around his throat as he wondered what on earth the police wanted with him.

"Yes, sir. Should I show him in?"

The Chief Science Advisor closed his eyes and sighed, "Alright Sandra, show him in would you." She nodded and hurried out of his office, leaving him briefly with his own thoughts. Russell rubbed his face tiredly and poured himself another drink. *It was starting to look like another of those days.*

The policeman that strode officiously into his office was Chief Inspector. Russell held out his hand awkwardly, "I'm sorry to have kept you waiting. I didn't realise."

"Chief Inspector Willis," he replied, brushing Russell's outstretched hand brusquely aside. "No need to apologise, I appreciate that you must be very busy. I'm sorry to disturb you, but I thought it was urgent that we speak."

"Yes?" asked Russell apprehensively.

"As you know, a member of your staff, a cleaner and his wife, have been found dead." The Chief Inspector took the seat opposite Russell's, uninvited. "At this time, we're treating their deaths as suspicious."

"I see," remarked Russell uncertainly. "And how does this concern me exactly?"

"The husband worked here, in this very building. This is supposedly a secure and secret location. I believe that their deaths could be linked to a possible attempt at espionage."

"Espionage?" repeated Russell with a growing sense of concern.

"Correct," confirmed the Chief Inspector. "I thought you should be made aware of the potential threat."

"I see," replied Russell, trying to maintain a disinterested look. "Well, I appreciate your bringing this to my attention, it does sound most troubling. But really, I think you need to talk to one of our security chaps by the sounds of it."

Removing his cap and placing it on his folded knee, the Chief Inspector stared at Russell impassively. He hadn't risen through the ranks of the Met without learning a thing or two about interviewing people. Willis often found it helpful to just wait and watch when conducting an interview or an interrogation. In fact, he treated all his daily interactions with people like that. His job and the uniform usually did the rest, as the pressure to confess was imbued into his unfortunate interreges.

Interpreting the look on the Chief Inspector's face incorrectly, Russell switched tact. "Unless of course, you want my direct assistance for some reason, Chief Inspector Willis? I'm happy to assist of course, if I can, within the purview of my job, obviously. Certain aspects of my work are restricted. Security reasons, you understand?"

Wiping an imaginary speck from an unblemished shoe, the Chief Inspector nodded curtly in the Chief Science Advisor's direction and smiled. "Can I ask if there is there something specific that's led you to my door?" pleaded Russell, feeling suddenly compelled to comply with the other man's wishes. "I'd like to know how I can help."

"Are you aware of any recent security breaches?" asked the Chief Inspector, placing his cap back on and standing up as he took further control of the one-sided conversation. "Something that may be linked to their deaths?" queried Willis. "Maybe something amiss or perhaps out of the ordinary?"

Russell shrugged his shoulders helplessly, unable to offer a reply. "I'd like to see where the cleaner worked, if that's possible?" persisted the Chief Inspector.

Russell shook his head. "Regretfully, I can't allow you to view the secure area where the late employee worked. Our security is extremely tight as I'm sure you'll appreciate. Even your clearance levels aren't enough to access the whole of this building, Chief Inspector. As I said, you'd need to talk with our security chaps and reach some sort of agreement for that type of thing. Although

I have to say, I don't fancy your chances much. They're a funny bunch that lot, and suspicious as hell."

The Chief Inspector pursed his lips as if to say something. He paused as Russell interjected, "I'm not personally aware of any breaches in our security. And certainly, I'm unaware of anything relating to anyone's death, Chief Inspector. We take great care to run a tight operation and minimise any risks where we possibly can."

Feeling more confident on familiar ground, Russell fell back on familiar habits and lapsed into Civil Service speak. "I don't think it'd be actually permissible for me to help you work around our security measures. That is, even if I could help you. Obviously, I really can't."

They exchanged a long uncomfortable look as the Chief Inspector struggled to decode the meaning behind the Chief Science Advisor's thoughts. Finally, Russell stood up and held out his hand, "Well, thank you for bringing this to my attention Chief Inspector Willis. I wish you the best of luck with your investigation. Of course, I'll inform you immediately if I discover anything that could be linked to their deaths. But I can't imagine that we've suffered a breach here. Otherwise, we'd already know about it. Thank you again for bringing this to my attention, I value your decision to keep me in the loop."

Unused to being dismissed, the Chief Inspector appraised him quizzically before taking his outstretched hand. "Very well, Mr. Russell. Thank you for taking the time to meet with me today."

Russell smiled nervously and watched him leave from behind the sanctity of his desk. He downed what was left in his glass and placed a call to the Minister's Principal

Private Secretary. Any departmental departures or deaths had to be reported to the Civil Service, they'd deal with this matter and Chief Inspector Willis from here on out.

As he hung up the phone, relieved at having moved the matter on, Russell toyed with the idea of letting the Defence Chief know of the Chief Inspector's concerns. But a flash of lightning outside made him hurriedly seek safety behind his desk. *One never knew for sure where electricity was involved*, he reminded himself. And so instead, he made off for the canteen. There was safety in numbers, Russell reasoned, his phobia of being struck by lightning dictating his behaviour.

Outside, the Chief Inspector took a last look up at the Chief Science Advisor's window. The man hadn't appeared to take his security concerns particularly seriously. Shaking his head wearily, Willis instructed his driver, "Take me back to headquarters." His driver nodded and started the car engine. Focused on their journey as they pulled away from the curb, neither of them noticed the car that discreetly followed behind. Curious as to their involvement and keeping its distance, the driver of the car tailed the Chief Inspector's vehicle.

NINETEEN

Velma pushed aside the stack of documents she'd been going through and yawned loudly. "Janice?" she bellowed. "What time is it?"

Her assistant flinched at the crack of thunder outside, shrieking as she hurried into the detective's office. Velma cackled with laughter whilst an embarrassed Janice smoothed down her skirt and said primly, "It's six-thirty, why?"

The detective's shoulders were still shaking with laughter as she said, "Could you be a dear and call Douglas, please? Ask him to meet me outside Queensway tube station, will you?"

Janice harrumphed, feigning annoyance at Velma's laughter. But she loved the raucous sound of Velma's laughter. Smirking, she asked, "What time shall I say, boss?"

"Seven-thirty should be fine," replied Velma. "You know I hate it when you call me that, Janice," she intoned, stuffing a sheaf of papers into her purse.

"I know," laughed Janice, winking at her.

Velma grinned good-naturedly, "Tell him that I might have a lead." She held out her hand for an umbrella from the well-stocked stand by the office door.

"Is there one in particular you're after?" Janice asked, her hand poised mid-air.

"The purple one dear," replied Velma.

"It might be prudent if I came with you. What do you think?" Janice followed up.

"There's no need for you to come with me. You can go home if you like."

"I really don't mind," Janice volunteered. "I've got nothing on tonight apart from a large basket of ironing."

Velma smiled sympathetically, "For our sins Janice, we all have to do our chores. I'll see you bright and early tomorrow morning, don't be late."

"Morning? Early? Are you sure that you're feeling all right Miss Scott?"

"Eleven is fine," replied Velma with a smile. "I know it's a little earlier than usual, but it's still a civil time to conduct our kind of business. And I was thinking that we could finish a little earlier too." Janice nodded, cheered by the idea of an earlier finish.

"It's an opportunity for you to go out, Janice. You could go dancing or something. I know that you still pine for Edward, but he's been dead a long time, and he's not coming back. Janice, you need to get yourself some sort of social life. I don't want you wasting away in the office or stuck at home. You're a pretty young thing and should get out more. The world won't wait for you, you have to get out there whilst you can and grab what you want."

"Have you been reading those American self-help books again?" asked Janice dubiously.

"The working hours thing is a good idea, isn't it?" persisted Velma, unperturbed. "I read about it in a magazine at the dentist of all places. It's called flexible working. What do you think? I think it'll catch on."

***

Douglas huddled underneath the detective's umbrella as a light drizzle fell around them. "Janice called me and asked me to meet you here. She said you had a lead?"

The detective nodded, "Do you see the office building across the street?" He peered over at the building opposite and nodded. "I suspect that somewhere inside there Douglas, are the answers to at least a few of your questions."

The reporter looked at her expectantly, "What makes you think that? Who works there?" She slipped her arm through his and hurried them across the street. They paused outside the marble steps and tried to peer into the foyer. He looked at her cryptically, "Well?"

"This is a government building," she explained. "Unfortunately, I doubt that they'll let us just stroll in. However, I'm interested in someone who is just about to come out." Douglas waited for her to say more, but she remained focused on the revolving door of the building. "Ah-ha," she whispered triumphantly, as a rotund figure emerged. The detective's grip on his arm tightened, "Just follow my lead, Douglas."

They loitered in the doorway until the man passed by, and then they began to follow him. "Who is he?" hissed the reporter. She didn't reply, instead, Velma quickened her pace.

"Keep up," she insisted. "I'm hoping he'll pop in for a drink somewhere before he heads home." Douglas nodded as they struggled to keep up with the rapidly disappearing figure.

They raced after him and turned a corner as the man ducked into a small, mock-Tudor pub. The detective brought them to an abrupt stop outside. "Wait here," she ordered, leaving Douglas holding her purple lady's umbrella. He watched her curiously as she followed the man inside. The reporter grinned to himself, *That poor chap doesn't know what he's in for.*

Velma glanced furtively in the man's direction as he waited impatiently to be served at the bar. She sidled up alongside him, "The service is a bit slow in here tonight isn't it?" The figure turned to look at her and smiled tensely. "Do you think you could do a lady a favour and order me whisky and soda whilst I visit the powder-room?" she asked, pressing a pound note into the surprised man's hands.

"I don't see why not," he replied pleasantly, gesturing to the barman.

"You're a sweetheart," she cooed, pecking him on the cheek. Velma dashed off in the direction of the lavatory and pretended to go inside. The detective checked that no one was looking and then slipped out through the back door of the pub. She raced around the corner and greeted Douglas with a grin.

"It's definitely him," she confirmed, snatching her umbrella from the reporter's hand. "I want you to come inside and hover by the door. Don't say anything, just try and look menacing, alright?"

Douglas frowned at her, "What do you mean?"

She patted his cheek fondly, "I want you to block the entrance, my dear. I'm going to try and persuade him that you're after me; that I'm in some sort of trouble. We have to find a way to get him in our corner."

The reporter shook his head doubtfully, "Can't we just ask him?"

Velma grinned, "But my way is so much more fun, Douglas. Come on, you really don't have to do anything other than stand at the door and occasionally look in my direction. The devil's in the detail, so don't smile when you go inside. Look mean and menacing."

He sighed and gave in. Douglas was rapidly learning that it was utterly pointless to try and reason with her. "Where should we meet afterwards?"

"Meet me in the café by the tube station," she replied. "I'll fill you in once I learn something. Just give me another five minutes before you come inside. I want to try and establish a rapport first."

"A rapport?" asked Douglas, wondering where on earth her scheme was going.

"It's already begun," she replied sweetly. "He just doesn't know it yet!"

The reporter's grin lapsed into a sympathetic smile as she hurried back inside the pub. Douglas was beginning to feel for the unfortunate fellow inside. *That poor bugger doesn't stand a chance.*

TWENTY

William Russell blinked with surprise as he received an unexpected peck on the cheek. "It's quite alright," he muttered awkwardly, sliding over Velma's drink and returning her money.

"That's very kind of you," remarked Velma, dazzling him with a generous smile. She tucked the pound note into her purse and sipped at her drink. "Let me reassure you. I don't frequent bars or ask strange men to buy me drinks," she said with a chuckle. Daintily, the detective held out her hand, "My name's Velma, what's yours?"

"Russell," he replied. "William Russell."

"Oh, I've known a few Williams in my time," she said. "They've always proved trustworthy. I'm lucky I found you, I have to say." He nodded uncertainly with no idea where this conversation was going. "Do you mind if I call you Bill?" she asked. Not waiting for a reply, Velma continued, "So what do you do? For a living, I mean?"

"Erm," he hesitated. "I suppose you could say that

I work for the Civil Service."

"That sounds like a demanding job. What department do you work in? I imagine that you're in a senior position. You look like the type of man who's good at managing things."

Russell blushed, he couldn't recall the last time he'd received any kind of praise. "Well, I suppose you could say that," he mumbled.

Velma's hand brushed against his as she asked, "Do you mind if we sit down? I've been on my feet all day, but I'd love to hear more about you and what you do."

"Of course, please forgive me," apologised Russell. "I'm utterly thoughtless." He removed his hat and coat from the adjacent stool, but Velma was already on her way to an empty table. Russell grabbed his belongings and his glass and hurried after her.

Velma thanked him as he pulled out a chair for her, "It's such a relief to meet a man with good manners these days. They're becoming increasingly rare, you know." Russell again turned crimson as he took the seat opposite hers. "So, you were telling me about your work?" she prompted.

He nodded with surprise "Yes, well, I wouldn't want to bore you."

"I doubt that's possible, Bill," Velma replied, fixing him with a winning smile. The government's Chief Science Advisor grinned back. *Maybe today wasn't going to be such a bad day after all.*

They talked for a few minutes, agreeably passing the time until he noted that Velma's face fell suddenly. He puzzled, *have I said something untoward?* Russell followed her gaze towards the pub's entrance. "Is there something wrong?" he asked, fervently hoping it wasn't something he'd said or done.

"It's that man over there," hissed Velma, sounding close to panic. "He's been following me around for the last few days. I don't know who he is or what he wants. But he's starting to make me feel nervous. What should I do?"

Russell eyed the loitering figure carefully. If he'd been at the office, it would have been a simple case of calling security. *He doesn't look too menacing*, Russell thought to himself, sizing up the other man. Velma clutched at his hand desperately, "Please Bill, can you help me?"

Russell patted her hand reassuringly, "I'll take care of this, my dear, now don't you worry." As he stood up, he sucked in his gut and headed towards the man who was now staring fiercely at him. Russell took a deep breath beforehand, he wasn't used to confrontation. He wondered what he was going to say as the distance between them grew smaller and smaller. Russell coughed nervously as he came toe to toe with Douglas Salter. "I say," he began. "You're making my friend extremely nervous. Why don't you just clear off?"

Douglas looked down at Russell and then over at the table where Velma was sitting. She was gesturing manically for him to leave. He gave Russell what he hoped was a withering look and hurried out of the pub trying not to laugh.

Russell was delighted. Even in his wildest dreams he hadn't expected things to go that smoothly. He suddenly felt a lot braver, and he turned to Velma and grinned triumphantly. With a newfound confidence, the government's Chief Science Advisor made his way back to the table. "Velma, my dear, I don't think you'll be having much trouble with him again."

The detective smiled enticingly, "You're so courageous, Bill. I don't know what I would have done if you weren't here."

Feeling invigorated and more confident than he had in years, Russell beamed as she looked up at him with doe eyes. He chuckled and replied, "I'm always happy to help out a damsel in distress."

TWENTY-ONE

The reporter smiled to himself as he wandered towards Westminster tube station. He wondered how Velma was getting on and grinned at the thought. *She really is a remarkable woman.* Douglas bought himself a newspaper and ducked inside the café next to the station. He ordered a slab of chocolate cake and a large milky coffee.

As he glanced over the other patrons he was startled to see Beeton glaring back at him. The intelligence officer folded his newspaper in two and stood up, heading towards Douglas's table. "Mr. Salter," he greeted him gruffly. "I do hope that your friend has relayed my message? It would be a nuisance to have to relay it once again."

Douglas stirred his coffee vigorously. He looked up at the squat-looking figure and replied, "Maybe you'd like to discuss why this is so important to you and your colleagues? Perhaps you'd like to comment on the record?"

Beeton bristled at the reporter's words. Not for the first time, he found Douglas Salter to be infuriatingly smug.

"Do you enjoy trouble?" he growled.

"Not at all," retorted the reporter. "But I am intrigued by the fact that you still appear to be following me around?"

"I'm just doing my job," replied Beeton. He kept his eyes firmly fixed on the reporter as he continued, "I'm keeping this country safe. What are you doing?"

Douglas laughed loudly, "What—from nosy reporters like me? Is that what you're inferring?" Beeton curled his lip in an approximation of a smile. It looked out of place on his worn countenance. "I doubt that you're privy to all the facts, Mr. Beeton. In fact, I can assure you of that. Why don't you go and confer with your superiors? You might find that they're prepared to fill you in."

A frown crossed the intelligence officer's face and he snarled, "I'd prefer it, Mr. Salter, if you'd just simply shut up and mind your own business."

The reporter pointed towards the door dismissively, "I certainly didn't ask you to join me, you can leave whenever you like. This is still a free country, last I heard."

Venomously, Beeton glared at him, fighting the urge to give the reporter a bloody nose. "I really hope we don't cross paths too often, Mr. Salter. It could prove to be a painful experience for you."

Undeterred by the intelligence officer's threat, the reporter replied, "Perhaps you could stop following me around then, my friends too. It makes it all the more difficult to avoid each other, don't you think?"

At a loss for words, Beeton ground his teeth. He was really starting to loathe Douglas Salter. He was too smart for his own good. "What an unexpected surprise," cut in the voice of the detective. "I do hope that you're not bothering Mr. Salter again, Frank." He turned to face her, as the café's patrons did their best to ignore the rising tension. "It would be unfortunate if I had to give you a matching black eye," she warned. "I mean, how could you maintain a low profile looking like that? It would certainly make you more conspicuous and it could even blow your cover!" She laughed breezily, "In fact, people might start to suspect that a panda had escaped from the zoo."

Douglas hid a grin behind his hand as Beeton mumbled awkwardly, "I was just leaving." A guffaw escaped the reporter's mouth before he could restrain it, and he desperately looked away as the intelligence officer glared at him.

The detective nodded curtly and held open the door of the café. "I'll be seeing you then, Frank." Furiously, he stomped outside, cursing under his breath. He was utterly sick of the pair of them. Velma smiled at her client as she took the chair facing him. "Really Douglas, you shouldn't goad him like that."

"I can't help it," he replied, shrugging his shoulders helplessly. "There's something about him that makes it impossible to resist."

The detective chuckled and ordered a pot of tea from the waitress. "You don't mind, do you, Douglas? I'm completely parched."

The reporter shook his head and ordered another coffee and two more slabs of cake. "Well, what happened in the pub? Did you get what you needed?"

Velma clapped her hands delightedly. "It went swimmingly, Mr. Salter. I've discovered some rather intriguing aspects to your case. I think that you'll be pleasantly surprised." He raised his eyebrows expectantly. "Just let me have a bite of this delicious-looking chocolate cake first," she began. "And then I'll tell you all about it." Douglas nodded, and happily trowelled another helping into his own salivating mouth.

A tall slender figure watched them surreptitiously from across the café. His features were hidden by the newspaper that he held taut in front of his face. *How interesting*, he mused to himself, as Velma and Douglas began to gossip like eager school girls.

TWENTY-TWO

Harold Cage glowered at the Minister as he hung up the telephone. He'd listened in to the call and wasn't happy at what he'd heard. "What do you think you're doing?" he barked. "You don't make policy decisions without my say-so. Do I need to remind you of how things work around here?"

The Minister rolled his eyes with exasperation. He was rapidly tiring of the self-important Chief who was constantly demanding his compliance. "Let me remind you, Mr. Cage, I'm the Minister of this department, not you. If things go wrong, it's my head on the chopping board—not yours."

Cage's face turned purple. "How dare you speak to me like that. I've served in this position for over ten years. And let me tell you, I've watched countless ministers come and go in that time. And for the most part, they've been a damn site more competent than you.

"Surely you mean compliant?" countered the Minister. "Perhaps that's why they've all come and gone whilst you've remained in situ." The Defence Chief's eyes started to bulge, he couldn't believe the insolence he was hearing. "Your position is secure isn't it?" persisted the Minister. "Essentially, you're accountable to no one. Whilst I serve at the Prime Minister's discretion."

Speechless, Cage got up and walked stiffly out of the Minister's office. He slammed the door shut and marched briskly towards the Cabinet Secretaries' office. He didn't care what it took. He was going to demand an immediate cabinet reshuffle and the Minister's head.

***

Russell hung up the telephone and grinned. He couldn't remember the last time he'd enjoyed himself so much. Humming to himself, he called in his secretary and told her she could go home early. As the office door closed, his brief moment of happiness was shattered as the telephone rang shrilly. His face fell as he listened, the Minister speaking rapidly down the line.

Russell hung up and morosely poured himself a large drink, downed it, and poured himself another. Cage was going to be furious when he heard of the Minister's instructions. *Who'd have thought he had the balls?* Russell wondered to himself. He couldn't believe that the Minister had chosen to make a power grab. And into the Defence Chief's realm, of all places. The Minister had decided that if he was going to carry the can for the project, then he was going to oversee it as well. Rubbing tiredly at his eyes as he chewed over the Minister's intentions, the government's Chief Science Advisor sighed loudly.

As he speculated over the impact of the Minister's decision, Russell looked over at his office door and speculated as to whether he could slip out of his office unnoticed. He jumped, as the door flew suddenly open, and the Defence Chief bustled in angrily. *Bloody hell*, he thought, when he saw the look of pure venom on the man's face. He's already heard.

Red-faced, Cage stomped towards Russell. "I'm demanding a cabinet reshuffle," he growled. "Can I count on your support?"

The Chief Science Advisor shrugged helplessly, "It's not my place to get involved in that side of things. And I don't really have any influence in that regard either. I'm afraid that I'm not the right person to ask. You really need to speak with the Cabinet Secretary."

Helping himself to a large whisky from Russell's store he retorted, "I bloody well know that. But he's not in his office right now. I'm canvassing support in the meantime. Can I count on you, Russell?"

Normally, William Russell would have acquiesced to the bullying tactics of the Defence Chief in an instant. But today he felt unusually emboldened after the previous day's encounter in the pub. The government's Chief Science Advisor surprised both the Defence Chief and himself by standing his ground. "As I said, it's not my place. You'll have to speak with the Cabinet Secretary."

The Defence Chief's face suddenly took on a colour Russell hadn't seen before. "You know, you really don't look at all well, Mr. Cage. Perhaps you should pay a visit to the Surgeon General's office instead?"

"Why you insolent little shit!" Spittle began to fly

from Cage's mouth as he unleashed a torrent of abuse towards the Chief Science Advisor. Russell stood up from behind his desk, "I'm going," he announced calmly to the astonished Defence Chief. "I have a prior engagement."

Left suddenly alone in Russell's office, Cage sagged helplessly into one of the worn leather chairs. *What's happening here? Why am I losing control?* Glumly, he helped himself to another whisky and pondered his next course of action.

TWENTY-THREE

Janice looked up from her trashy romance novel as the shrill ring of the telephone sounded. "Hello? Velma Scott detective agency—how can I help you?" she trilled robotically.

"It's me, Janice," replied Douglas. "I wondered if you fancied going out for a drink after work?"

An enthusiastic smile crossed her face, "I'd love to, Douglas," she gushed. "Where shall we meet?"

Relieved that she hadn't turned him down, the reporter replied, "I can pick you up from the office if you like." Unable to resist, he told her the news, "And by the way, Miss Scott has an actual date."

"A date?" balked Janice incredulously, her eyebrows shooting up with astonishment. In the five years she'd worked for the detective, not once could she ever recall her going on a date. "Are you sure you've got that right, Douglas?"

Chuckling, he replied, "Well it appears that her ruse in the pub worked even better than she dared. That chap from the government, Russell, he seems quite keen. You won't believe it Janice, but she's actually quite dizzy."

"Dizzy? Miss Scott?" replied Janice, shaking her head with bewilderment.

Douglas laughed, "It's a sight alright. She's canvassed my opinion on six different hats already. I really can't take anymore. I'm heading over now, is that alright with you?"

The image he described made Janice giggle. "I can't wait, Douglas. I'll see you soon." She waited for him to hang up first, and then raced into the bathroom with her purse. Emptying its contents onto the shelf, she began to apply her makeup.

***

William Russell bought a large bouquet of flowers from a nearby stall and straightened his tie. He checked his appearance awkwardly in the reflection of a shop window and waited anxiously.

Velma smiled as she rounded the corner and saw him. She waved cheerily, and excitedly he waved back. The detective wore a slim-fitting, floor-length evening gown slit-high at one leg. Emerald green in colour, she matched it with an eccentric-looking combination of what looked like former soldier's boots and a hazel brown beret, which she perched precariously on the top of her head. Pressing the bouquet of flowers into her hands, he bowed slightly, "I'm delighted that you called, Velma. I really wasn't expecting it."

Fidgeting with her hair, Velma blushed, "You

didn't think I was too, forward did you?"

Russell's own cheeks were already flushed with colour as he shook his head, "Not—at—all, my—dear," he laboured.

She beamed brightly and squeezed his arm as she took hold of it. "I'll buy the first round of drinks tonight. And then we'll see where we go from there shall we?"

Brushing his hand gently across her cheek, he whispered, "What I should have said was that I found your approach refreshing. In fact, I should have said that you quite took my breath away, Miss Scott."

Flushing at his words, she held her breath as he continued. "I've never really understood what women look for in a man," he admitted. "And I'd abandoned all hope of ever meeting one that liked me, for who I am."

Guiltily, she replied, "You're putting a lot of pressure on a first date, Bill," as they loitered outside the door. The disheartened look that crossed his face made her feel even guiltier. She'd taken a shine to him and it had caught her by surprise. Velma broke the awkward moment by winking at him and asking, "Are we doing this then Mr. Russell? Are we going to trip the light fantastic in all of the pubs near Whitehall?"

Grinning with delight, he added, "I'm sorry Velma. What I meant to say is that I was delighted when you called. I tend to get tongue-tied around gorgeous women. Well, by most women actually…But I don't with you for some reason, and it's not that I don't find you attractive. Because I do, by the way." She frowned as he tried to herd her towards the door. "What I should have said was that you brought a little sunshine into an otherwise grey and tedious day; so thank you dearly for that, Velma."

Her frown changed to a smile, "You should have led with that one," she chuckled.

Laughing, Russell nodded and patted her hand fondly as he held open the door, "After you, my dear." She squeezed his hand and stepped inside the pub where they'd met the night before. Russell took a hopeful deep breath and followed in after her.

***

Huddled in a doorway across the street from the shady old pub, Beeton smirked. He finally had some information that the Defence Chief might be interested to learn. He'd failed so far in locating his primary target. But this liaison between the Chief Science Advisor and the detective could be construed as disloyalty; perhaps even treachery. Beeton began to view his report to Cage the following morning with a little less apprehension. In fact, from what he'd just seen, he might escape one of Cage's legendary tongue lashings altogether. Happily, he headed home whistling loudly as he walked.

TWENTY-FOUR

Douglas gradually came around and found himself tied to a hard wooden chair. Each of his arms and legs were restrained by a series of leather straps. They bit deep into his flesh, causing him to wince as he struggled to stem the rising sense of panic. His predicament caused him to eventually stop, and instead, he tried to make out his surroundings, which appeared musty, cold, and dark.

Something sat crowned uncomfortably over the top of his head. It prevented him from moving his head and forced his eyelids open, not allowing him to even blink.

Uncomprehendingly, he stared ahead—it was impossible to do anything else. The reporter felt nauseous and more than a little alarmed in the disoriented state in which he found himself.

His body suddenly tensed at the scraping sound he heard somewhere behind him. A crack of light crept over the concrete floor. Douglas gasped as he fleetingly caught a glimpse of his reflection in a pool of muddy water.

The contraption he was wearing over his head appeared to be composed of a series of interlocking wires. It reminded him of something he'd seen once in a museum—a medieval torture device. Shuddering at the memory, he held his breath as he heard the shuffle of footsteps. The spindle of light suddenly vanished, and he was plunged back into darkness. Douglas grimly stared ahead, eyelids fixed open.

A moment later, a dull whir started as a projector motor began to run. A large cinema-style screen suddenly flickered into life, and he was surprised that he hadn't noticed it before. Somewhere above him, a beam of light hit the grubby surface of the screen.

A series of images flashed before his eyes. Douglas fervently wished that he could look away or simply shut his eyes. Denied by the device on his head, the smouldering intensity of the images seared themselves into his mind. One after another, depictions of gruesome acts of violence shimmered before him. Feeling increasingly agitated in his bleak surroundings, eyes pried open by the contraption on his head, Douglas had no choice but to stare at the screen. He had no concept of time, and apart from the sound of his own laboured breathing and the whir of the motor, it was forebodingly quiet.

The monstrous images continued to unrelentingly flash before his eyes. Grimacing at what he was forced to watch, his body grew taut as adrenalin coursed through his body.

Gradually, he became distracted by a whimpering sound from somewhere in the room. As he grew accustomed to the noise, he finally realised that the sounds were emanating from himself, he was crying. Douglas attempted to clear his throat in an attempt to regain some sort of control. Finally, the sound of the motor slowed, and the images suddenly vanished, plunging him back into darkness.

Douglas gasped with relief and tried to compose himself. His breathing grew more measured, and the sound of his heart pounding became a little less intense. *What the hell's going on here?* he asked himself. Douglas didn't have time to think about it, the projector cranked back into life. The light focused on the screen again, and he found himself watching the same series of images on a loop. Fraught with anxiety, the reporter exhausted himself as he wrestled his restraints. Eventually succumbing, growing numb to what he was seeing, Douglas gave in and let the pictures and the eerie sense of helplessness wash over him.

TWENTY-FIVE

Fretfully, Janice glanced at the time as she paced around the office. She called Douglas's office again, but there was still no reply. Kicking off her heels with a frown, she sank despairingly into her chair, anxiously biting her lip as she wondered what to do. An unexpected rattle startled her, and Janice looked up as the lock on the office door clicked open. Velma sailed unevenly through the door. "What are you still doing here?" slurred the detective. "I thought Douglas was taking you out for the evening?"

"So did I," replied Janice sullenly. "I'm really quite worried about him."

Drunkenly, the detective scrutinised her assistant. She could make out where her assistant's mascara had run and vainly tried to reassure her. "It's not like Douglas to be late, he's very well-mannered. I'm sure it's nothing untoward. Perhaps he's just been delayed at work."

"But it's nine-thirty!" wailed Janice. "I've called his office and home several times. He hasn't picked up, and I really don't know what to do Miss Scott."

Velma slumped into the chair opposite and attempted to calm her assistant. "Take a deep breath, my dear. There's no point in wasting good tears over a man of all things."

Janice dabbed at her eyes with a handkerchief and nodded, "But after what happened with Mrs. Gladstone, I can't help but fear the worst."

The detective placed a reassuring arm around Janice's shoulder and squeezed tightly. "He'll turn up eventually. You mark my words." Janice smiled gratefully, feeling mollified, even if she wasn't entirely convinced. "If he doesn't turn up tomorrow," continued Velma, "I'll ask my new friend to look into it, alright?"

Janice nodded, she was starting to feel a little calmer. "He'd better have a good excuse for standing me up, Miss Scott."

"That's the attitude Janice," Velma declared. "Get your coat and I'll walk you home."

Wiping a tear from her cheek, Janice smiled and hugged the detective warmly. "Thanks, Miss Scott, I needed that."

"You're welcome, my dear," replied the detective warmly. "Why don't we have a quick drink before we call it a night? I think I can manage one more." Grinning, Janice hugged her again and fetched two teacups into which she poured two generous sherries.

"So, tell me about this new friend of yours."

"He's a rather nice fellow I just bumped into." Velma grinned at her wickedly, "When I say bumped into him, that's not entirely true…I'll tell you all about it on the way back to yours."

As they stepped out into the cool night air, Janice shivered. She looked up as the clouds wafted over the face of the moon, which hung low in the sky. "I do hope he's alright," she murmured.

"Of course, Douglas is alright," reassured Velma. "Men always are. Besides, if he's not, it's his own fault for standing you up in the first place." Giggling, Janice linked arms with the detective as they ambled down the street together.

TWENTY-SIX

Harold Cage listened to Beeton's report with an air of mild indifference. The only time he took note was when he mentioned the meeting between Russell and a woman named Scott. "Who is she?" he barked.

"She's a private investigator," Beeton replied, trying to mask the smugness in his voice. "I thought you might find it interesting, the fact that they'd met."

"And what of the remaining target I've asked you to locate? Have you made any progress?"

Beeton hesitated nervously, he'd hoped the news of Russell's encounter would appease the Defence Chief. "I'm still working towards that aim, sir. It's taking a little longer than anticipated."

"But you do know where they are?" reiterated Cage.

"I've established a general vicinity," agreed Beeton haltingly. "I just need another forty-eight hours to pin down an exact location."

"You can have twenty-four," agreed Cage graciously. "Don't let me down, Beeton."

"No, sir," he replied, feeling a surge of relief. "How would you like me to handle the Russell situation?"

Harold Cage smiled thinly, "You can leave that with me."

Beeton waited for the Defence Chief to say something further, but the line remained quiet. "Well, if there's nothing else, sir?"

"That'll be all," replied Cage before he hung up.

The intelligence officer breathed a sigh of relief and stepped out of the phone box. His face dropped as he came face-to-face with the detective. Finding her there, waiting for him, proved a little unnerving. "Miss Scott?" he remarked gruffly. "What are you doing here?"

"It's about Douglas Salter," she replied. "He appears to be missing and as you've been keeping tabs on him, I wondered if you had anything to do with his disappearance?"

Beeton attempted to suppress a large grin, "You say he's missing?" The detective nodded and studied him closely trying to gauge his response. "Well, it's nothing to do with me. I can assure you of that, Miss Scott."

"I see," she replied. "And do you have any idea as to who else might have an interest in our mutual friend?"

The intelligence officer shook his head, "I'm afraid not, and even if I did, I wouldn't be at liberty to divulge that kind of intel."

She held his gaze and wondered whether to try and press any further. "I'm very good friends with his editor, you know. I doubt it would go down well if a story were to appear about a missing journalist. One whose disappearance could be linked to the Intelligence Services…I do hope you'll decide to keep me informed Frank, if you do hear anything. I wouldn't want to have to make another missing person's report, you see?"

Choosing to ignore the implied threat, Beeton replied, "I bet you wish that I'd kept my eye on him a little longer now, eh Miss Scott?"

The detective smiled back disarmingly, "I imagine your superiors might agree with that sentiment as well. Because it would be unfortunate if whatever it is they think he knows were to fall into unfriendly hands, wouldn't it?"

The smirk vanished from Beeton's face as her words sunk in. He nodded reluctantly, "I'll let you know if I hear anything."

The detective smiled sweetly, "I'm glad you've decided to cooperate. It'd be a shame to take the matter any higher. I'm not sure if it would reflect on you very well. I'll expect a call from you, Frank, tomorrow will be fine." She held his gaze a moment longer than necessary and then turned on her heel.

Left floundering, Beeton watched her disappear into the distance. *Bloody hell*, he thought to himself as it crossed his mind that Defence Chief Cage might have had some involvement in the journalist's disappearance. Knowing him and his reputation as he did, he certainly wouldn't put it past him.

TWENTY-SEVEN

Douglas Salter was surprised to find himself looking down at his own body from a height. Physically, he appeared to be still strapped to the chair. But he noted a distant expression on his face, as his eyes stared lifelessly at the images projected onto the cinema screen. Disconcertingly, he began to wonder if he was dead.

Shaking aside the thought, he incredulously turned in mid-air and found himself hovering close to the ceiling of the room. He looked down again and traced the light from the projector to a small window which laid above and behind his limp figure.

Effortlessly, he floated over towards the window and peered inside. A small deserted room lay beyond the window. Douglas willed himself inside and somehow materialised beside the projector. He studied the mechanism, trying to find the off switch. He then realised that he didn't appear to have any fingers, or hands, or any means of disabling it at all.

Douglas felt that he should have been alarmed

by the fact that he had no material body to speak of. But instead, he felt completely at ease.

I told you that I'd help you, a voice whispered.

Startled, Douglas looked over his shoulder. "Hello?" he asked the empty room with an air of trepidation.

You've been put into a form of sleep. The voice patiently informed him. *A hypnologic state, as my carer used to refer to it.*

"Your carer?" repeated Douglas in confusion. "Where are you?" asked Douglas, still searching the room uncertainly. "Who are you?"

I'm Beatrice, the voice replied softly. *I was transformed into a state like the one you're experiencing now, shortly before my death. My physical death*, the voice corrected itself.

"You're a ghost?" asked Douglas, realising that he should have felt afraid. Instead, a deep-seated curiosity took root. The sound of light laughter filled his mind. "Am I also dead?"

Not yet, replied Beatrice liltingly. *I pulled you out before any real damage was inflicted.*

"I suppose I should thank you then," Douglas answered. "Where am I exactly? And how did I get here?"

When you were brought here, you were already unconscious. Drugged I suppose. Do you remember eating or drinking anything that tasted metallic?

The reporter thought he shook his head from side to side in reply, before realising that he didn't actually have a head to shake anymore. "No," he eventually replied. "I remember that I was on my way to see a friend…"

I imagine they have other methods of inducing sleep when they need to. I watched as you were bound to the chair and the device fitted to your head.

"Who are they? And perhaps I should have led with this first, but can you help me get out of here?"

I've elected to help you, the voice responded. *But I need your help in exchange.*

"I thought that you said you were already dead? How can I help you?"

You must prevent this from happening to others. You must hold those responsible to account.

"How on earth do I do that?"

The people responsible for my being like this and for your current situation are working towards the same goal. They performed similar experiments on you when you were a child. Just as they did to me and my children—don't you remember their faces?

Douglas shuddered involuntarily. In the room below, his body spasmed in unison. "I think perhaps I'd recognise their faces if I saw them again. But I don't know their names or even how to begin to track them down."

I can help you to find them, replied Beatrice. *We'll talk later, you're about to be probed.*

"Probed?" Douglas yelped with alarm.

Beatrice didn't reply. His mind swooped from its high vantage point and rushed back into his physical body. His throat croaked slightly, as a spindly figure jabbed him in the arm with a needle. "Wake up, Mr. Salter!"

The glazed look in his eyes faded, and Douglas started to focus on the man leering in front of him. He realised that the face looked vaguely familiar. "Come now, Mr. Salter. This is no time for you to be passing out. We have so much to catch up on."

"Who are you?" the journalist rasped as his vision slowly started to clear.

"Don't you remember? I really expected much more from you Douglas. You used to be one of my star pupils." He unclasped the device from the reporter's skull and Douglas blinked rapidly. His eyelids were bruised, and the lack of moisture caused his eyes to sting. Douglas stared up at the man's face and then immediately started to retch.

The memories which invaded his mind seemed uncontrollable. In a torrent, they rushed through every crevice of his brain. Nodding, the figure smiled at him cheerily. "I see that you're starting to remember. That's very good news. I'll leave you to process those thoughts for a while. Perhaps we'll talk later."

Douglas gargled something unintelligible in reply. He struggled violently against the restraints, trying to work them loose. It felt as if his mind was ablaze, like an uncontrollable bushfire. As he howled in agony, spittle flying down his chin, the spindly man chuckled. "Don't worry, my boy. We'll speak again soon." The sound of the man's footsteps receded, and the reporter screamed loudly. No one answered, he was all alone. Douglas broke into a fevered sweat and began to sob.

TWENTY-EIGHT

Janice looked tearfully at the detective. "There's still no sign of Douglas. Nobody knows where he is. I've called his editor and his colleagues. I've called his home. I really think we should report this to the police."

Velma held her assistant's morose gaze. "I'm not sure that'll help matters, Janice. We don't want to panic those who might have him. It could result in something unfortunate."

"Like what?" she sniffled. "What could be worse than this?" The telephone on her desk rang urgently and Janice rushed to pick it up. "Yes?" she answered in a fraught tone. "Yes," she said again, looking pointedly at Velma. "It's for you, Miss Scott. A Mr. Russell wants to know if you're available for dinner this evening?"

The detective blushed, "I'll take the call in my office, Janice. Please put him through would you," she said, scampering into the adjoining office. "Bill," she answered in a cheery tone. "What a lovely surprise to hear from you. How are you, my dear?"

"I'm all the better now for speaking with you" he chuckled. "Listen, I was wondering if you fancied going out for dinner tonight?"

"Oh Bill, I'd love to, but something has come up at work."

"I see," he replied, sighing disappointedly. "I thought we got on rather well last night,"

"We did!" exclaimed Velma, giggling. "It's just that one of my clients has gone missing. I'm rather concerned for his safety. Otherwise, it wouldn't be a problem."

"I understand," replied Russell sadly. "Duty comes first."

Velma hesitated, "Perhaps you could help me out, Bill? I wouldn't dare to ask if I didn't think it was important."

"Go on," he replied, eager to help. "If it'll aid you being free for dinner, I'll do it."

She giggled again, "You're a sweetie, Bill."

"Well, I do try to be," he agreed, good-naturedly.

"My client believed that his life was under threat. Normally I'd take stories like that with a pinch of salt, but I discovered that he was being followed by an intelligence officer from the security services," explained Velma.

"I see," Russell replied, intrigued.

"Now, I've already spoken with the intelligence officer in question. He calls himself Frank Beeton," she continued. "I'm unsure as to whether that's his real name, but he insisted that he had nothing to do with my client's disappearance. He also said that, to his knowledge, neither had any of the intelligence services. I was wondering if you could maybe pull a few strings? Try to find out discreetly if anyone knows anything?"

William Russell paused before finally answering in exasperation, "Good god woman. What the devil have you got yourself involved in?"

"I know it's a lot to ask Bill," Velma continued. "I won't take it personally if you don't want to get involved. To be honest, I really wouldn't blame you in the slightest."

The silence over the phone dragged before he finally replied, "Velma, what's the name of your client? And when and where were they last seen?"

"He's called Douglas," she responded. "Douglas Salter. He's a nice young chap, a newspaper reporter. My assistant, Janice is rather fond of him. They were supposed to go out for dinner last night, but he never turned up, and he hasn't appeared at work today either. Nobody has any idea of his whereabouts."

"I can see why you're worried," muttered Russell, making a note of the reporter's name. "Let me dig around a little. I'll call you back in a couple of hours, my dear."

"You're an angel," Velma replied delightedly. "I'll wait for your call, and Bill, thanks again for doing this. I know it's a lot to ask."

"I'll do my best," he said, already feeling uneasy at the prospect of dealing with the Defence Chief. "I can't promise you anything, but I will try to find out what's happened to your client."

"I couldn't ask for more, my darling. Thank you," cooed the detective.

They each waited for the other to hang up first until William Russell finally gave in and said softly, "Velma—I'll call you later, love…God bless."

The detective swooned and then hung up. She was certain that William Russell would be able to track down her missing client. "It's alright, Janice," she called out to her assistant, "My friend has agreed to help."

Janice poked her head around the door, "Has he heard anything?" she asked hopefully.

Velma shook her head, "Not yet, no. But I'm certain he can help."

"When will you hear from him?" fretted Janice.

"He said he'll call back in a few hours. He's going to ask around first. I'm positive that Douglas will turn up safe and sound. So do stop worrying, my dear. That frown you're carrying around with you will ruin that pretty face of yours."

Normally, Janice laughed at Velma's remarks about her appearance, but she was too anxious. Instead, she retreated from the detective's office and slumped into her chair behind the desk. *Douglas, where are you?* Anxiously, she stared at the phone on her desk, hoping for news.

TWENTY-NINE

arold Cage looked up with surprise as William Russell appeared unannounced in his office, bearing gifts. He placed two bottles of single malt on his desk and took the seat opposite. "Russell?" Cage muttered suspiciously. "I don't recall you ever visiting my office before. To what do I owe this pleasure?"

Russell smiled hesitantly, "Things have felt a little tense between us recently, and I thought that perhaps a fresh start might improve things? We are on the same side, after all."

Cage scrutinised his colleague warily, holding his gaze for an uncomfortably long time. "I can go along with that, Bill," he replied finally. Nodding with relief, Russell unscrewed the cap of the nearest bottle whilst the Defence Chief expectantly held out his glass. Filling Cage's glass past the halfway mark, Russell poured himself a much smaller measure. He sipped at it and then eased himself back into the worn brown leather chair.

"Well, what's happening in regards to the test

subjects? Has there been any progress locating them?" Russell quipped.

The Defence Chief frowned with annoyance.

"I'm just making conversation," interjected Russell hurriedly. He downed his drink to steady his nerves but refused to drop his line of questioning. "It'd be helpful to know, Harold. I have to order the equipment, and it makes no sense to spend the money if we don't actually have anyone to test it on."

Cage let his irritation dissipate and sighed. "There's nothing to report yet, Bill. Unfortunately, we've suffered a bit of a setback. One of our targets has been found dead. Well, murdered actually. We're looking into that, but I doubt it's related to our project."

Russell nodded, an anxious look spreading across his face. "Funny you should mention that, as I had a visit from the Chief Inspector recently. It seems that a member of our cleaning staff and his wife were found dead as well. I start to worry when coincidences begin to stack up like that."

"Were they murdered?" asked the Defence Chief, concern showing on his face. He didn't believe in coincidences either.

Russell shrugged uncertainly, "The Chief Inspector wanted to view the area the cleaner worked in. I refused, of course, but he did appear to suggest that perhaps espionage may have played a factor."

"Did he now?" Cage murmured. "You should have mentioned this to me earlier, Bill."

Russell paused before answering, "Well, it didn't seem relevant at the time. Not until you mentioned that one of our potential subjects had been found murdered. Do you think he was right, Harold? Do you really think their deaths are related somehow?"

Cage studied his colleague closely over the desk. Despite his reservations, this unexpected and collegial approach by Russell appeared to be reaping dividends. *You catch more flies with honey*, the Defence Chief reminded himself. "We all have ghosts of one shape or another, but I'll tell you what Bill, I'll look into it personally as you're a friend, and I'll be sure to let you know."

William Russell nodded conspiratorially. Seemingly happy to be taken into Cage's confidence, the Chief Science Advisor grinned.

The Defence Chief topped off his glass and smiled back chillingly. "Was there anything else?" Cage asked, watching as Russell nursed his scotch.

Russell stared uneasily at his drink. "Well, erm… There was one other thing," he ventured. "A Mr. Douglas Salter, he's a newspaperman. It appears he's disappeared. I wondered whether you could use your contacts to ascertain his whereabouts? You see, a friend of mine is rather concerned about his safety."

Cage arched his eyebrows with surprise, "Salter, you say?"

Russell sipped on his drink and nodded. Looking away quickly, he studied a mark on the floor, finding it suddenly very interesting. Noting his awkward behaviour, Cage asked, "Is this man Salter, a friend of yours Bill?"

Russell shook his head, "No, no. He's a friend of a friend. I just thought I'd ask, that's all…"

"Hmm, I see," replied Cage, musing over his next

choice of words. "Well, I can ask around if you'd like. In this new spirit of openness—does that sound alright with you?"

Russell nodded enthusiastically, "That'd be really helpful Harold, thank you."

The Defence Chief grinned, exposing a row of yellowing upper teeth. "It's my pleasure, Bill. I'll let you know the moment I hear of anything. Well, if that's everything, I really must be getting on."

Russell realised that he was being dismissed, and he stood up slightly woozily. "We should do this again," he said. Cage nodded pleasantly and escorted him towards his office door. Holding it open, he watched as the government's Chief Science Advisor staggered out into the corridor.

"I'm surprised to say that I enjoyed our little conversation, Bill." Russell turned awkwardly and waved, before embarking up the stairwell at the end of the corridor. The Defence Chief smirked and shut the door. "A friend of a friend," he snorted derisively.

Checking his watch beforehand, Cage reached for the telephone on his desk, "Beeton?" he barked.

"Yes, sir," replied Beeton, feeling apprehensive at the unexpected call from his boss. "I hear that the reporter, Salter, has disappeared. Do you know anything about it?"

"No, sir. It's got nothing to do with me."

"I want you to look into it," pressed Cage. "I think it's a little odd that he vanishes just as he's been warned off, don't you?"

"Well, yes, I suppose so, sir," Beeton replied sullenly. For most of the day, he'd enjoyed the idea of Douglas

Salter enduring a beating by some nefarious underworld figure. Saving the reporter from a deserved thrashing really didn't sound that appealing to him.

"One other thing, Beeton…"

"Yes, sir?"

"I'm surprised to find you at home at this hour. I take it that you've located the remaining target?"

"Yes, I've located him," replied Beeton hastily. "He's based up in Scotland. I popped home to grab an overcoat before I caught a train up there."

"Very good," replied Cage. "I'll expect your report soon, I imagine?"

"Yes, sir."

"Good hunting," responded Cage in an unexpectedly friendly tone.

Beeton gulped nervously, the Defence Chief's sudden change of tack filled him with mortal dread. "Thank you, sir," he replied worriedly; the concern visibly etched into his brow the longer the call continued.

THIRTY

Douglas Salter stirred uneasily. His hopes faded as he found himself still restrained and tied to a chair. The reporter's eyes stung from the glaring light which had etched itself onto his retinas. Unable to look away or even to blink, tears streamed without restraint down his cheeks. "I see that you're finally awake, Mr. Salter," spoke a triumphant-sounding voice.

He tried to reposition his body to locate where it had come from, but it was useless. *There's no point in struggling, it isn't time,* intoned a disembodied voice. Douglas held his breath, the voice he heard in his mind was the one that had spoken to him earlier. She'd called herself Beatrice, and she had claimed to be able to help him.

"Get me out of here!" demanded Douglas frantically.

The first voice, the man's voice, laughed harshly. "I'm not convinced that you're quite ready yet. Perhaps another few days, and then we'll see, Mr. Salter." The sound of footsteps echoed softly as the man departed. A switch flicked somewhere, and the searing light suddenly blinked off, leaving him with bright spots dancing in front of his eyes.

Douglas sighed wearily as the oppressive darkness began to encroach. *Are you ready?* asked the disembodied voice of Beatrice. *This isn't going to be easy. You'll have to move quickly if you're to escape.*

"Ready?" repeated Douglas under his breath. He was starting to wonder if he was losing his mind. Eventually, he decided even that was preferable to remaining where he was. "I'm ready," he finally answered, not entirely convinced that anyone was hearing him.

Good. Now I want you to pull against your restraints. Pull them taut, as tight as you possibly can. Wordlessly, he obeyed the voice's instructions and yanked hard.

He strained against the straps until they bit into the flesh of his wrists and ankles. As he struggled, the leather noose around his neck tightened. Initially, he was too busy choking to notice anything happening. Convinced that he was about to black out from asphyxiation, the straps around his neck suddenly loosened and then snapped. His head fell forward onto his chest, and greedily he gulped down gasps of air.

Don't stop now, warned Beatrice's voice shrilly. *Pull against the restraints, harder. I can't do this on my own. I need your help.* Again, he obeyed, and Douglas pulled against his restraints until he was sure that his shoulders would pop out of their sockets.

Sweat poured down his brow as he struggled. Douglas couldn't be sure, but he could have sworn that he sensed a nibbling sensation somewhere near his wrists.

He shivered at the thought but continued to pull, swearing that he could hear the slow snapping of individual twines. Screaming with exertion as he struggled, his hands suddenly broke free.

Still gasping for breath, his numb fingers struggled with the contraption over his head. He tore at the wires, ripping them from his scalp alongside clumps of hair. Urgently, his hands moved down to the restraints around his ankles. He pulled at them desperately, determined that he wouldn't stay another minute.

Deliberately, he worked himself free and uneasily staggered to his feet. He felt dizzy as he stood, and his legs refused to obey his commands. *Hurry up!* urged Beatrice. *There's a ladder at the far end of the room. Climb up and get onto the roof.*

Douglas mindlessly obeyed the instructions and stumbled across the room in the dark. His bruised fingers felt along the wall at the far side until they grasped something solid; the ladder Beatrice had promised. *You're running out of time,* she urged as he heaved himself up, rung by rung.

It felt like an eternity as he climbed higher and higher. Finally, Douglas clambered onto a narrow wooden platform at the top. A door creaked somewhere below him. He held his breath at the sound of approaching footsteps while a figure entered the room. His heart pounded in his chest. It was so loud that he became convinced the figure below would hear it and look straight up at him.

Agitated yelps rang out as two more figures rushed urgently into the room. "Find him!" barked the spindly figure. "He can't have gotten far." Douglas watched nervously from his perch up in the rafters of the building. Imperiously, the figure looked about himself and then strode stork-like out of the room below.

Douglas rolled onto his back and let out a sigh of relief. *It's not over yet,* warned the disembodied voice of Beatrice. *You've still got to escape. Now, make your way over to the opposite side of the roof.*

He didn't argue or even really think about it. Instead, Douglas did exactly as the voice guided. He eased himself from rafter to rafter, ignoring the perilous drop below and instead focused on a single goal: escape.

You're doing well, prompted the voice as he neared the opposite side of the building.

Douglas nodded. The voice told him what to do next. *Do you see the rotten planks in front of you? Just work your way through them, you're nearly there.* The reporter scratched at them with his fingernails until they bled, picking loose the damp fragments of wood. *Hurry!* urged the voice in his mind.

Desperately, Douglas tore at the splintering shards until he could just make out a single shaft of moonlight in the sky. Feeling invigorated, he shoved hard with his shoulder against the gap. The crack of snapping wooden panels echoed as he fell through onto the outside of the roof. Breathing heavily, Douglas warily stole a view down below him. There was no sign of his captors, *Climb down and run. Run for your life, Douglas.*

He didn't argue, the reporter scrambled down a rusty, iron drainpipe and landed heavily on a muddy patch of ground alongside the rundown warehouse. He staggered to his feet, his legs felt as though they were made of lead.

Frantic, he began to run, urging himself on and ignoring the feeling that his lungs felt like they would burst at any moment. Fear and adrenaline motivated his desperate escape as he continued to flee deeper and deeper into the night.

THIRTY-ONE

Beeton shivered in the cold winter air as he disembarked from the train. The clock in the station read nine-thirty and it was dark and drizzly. The train accelerated with a shrill whistle and the plumes of smoke wrapped themselves around Beeton like a cloak while he waited on the platform.

His breath clouded in front of his face, and he shoved both hands into his pockets against the chill of the night air. "Mr. Beeton?" a voice called as a figure slipped out from the shadows.

The intelligence officer whirled around with surprise and noted a man approaching him from the door of the ticket office. "Yes—that's me," he replied, feeling the reassuring weight of his pistol inside his coat pocket.

The man nodded a quick greeting. "I've been asked to take you to your destination. Mr. Cage asked me to see to it personally. If you'll just follow me, we can take my car."

Grudgingly, Beeton weighed the figure up. The

man was tall, thin, and appeared to be in his early fifties. Pale-skinned with clear blue eyes, silver flecks of grey dotted his hair and beard. "I wasn't aware that Mr. Cage had made any such request?" he replied suspiciously.

The man shrugged helplessly. "I just do what I'm told," he replied simply.

Beeton studied him curiously and nodded, "Alright Mr...?"

"McLeish," the man answered with a wry smile.

"Very well, Mr. McLeish, please lead the way."

The man nodded in reply and turned on his heel. Warily, Beeton kept a firm grasp on his revolver in his coat pocket and followed after him. As they left the station, he struggled to remember a single instance of Cage ever making his job any easier. Something about this just didn't feel right. Keeping his eyes firmly fixed on the departing figure, he weighed his options.

As Beeton neared the waiting car, its engine was already running. Regardless of who this man was, he decided that it was too good an opportunity to miss from an intelligence gathering perspective. He took a deep breath and clambered in, pulling the door shut behind him.

The man smiled at him humourlessly and flicked on the car's headlights. Slowly, they pulled away from the station. Alert to danger, Beeton kept a watchful eye on the driver. "Aren't you going to ask me where we're headed?" he asked as the car crept down the narrow, unlit road.

"There's no need," replied the driver. "There's only one road from the train station, and it goes into town. I've booked you a room in the local pub. You can stay there tonight, and we'll move out in the morning." Beeton wasn't sure how to respond. This seemed far too well drilled for an intelligence job. "Don't you worry Mr. Beeton, I'll get you to where you need to be."

That's what's worrying me, the intelligence officer thought as the car whistled down the road. *I don't even know where I'm going myself.* McLeish turned to him and smiled broadly. "You'll be fine once you've had a few drinks. It'll all start to make sense then."

Surprised, Beeton nodded without replying. Feeling distinctly uneasy, he turned to stare out of the window as the driver chuckled and hit the accelerator. The car lurched forward and Beeton returned his attention to the driver, "I'm not in such a hurry that we need to risk an accident," he muttered. Ignoring his protests, the driver pushed down harder on the pedal, and the engine howled mercilessly. The intelligence officer grimaced and finally began to wonder what he'd actually gotten himself embroiled in.

THIRTY-TWO

Velma checked her watch whilst she waited for William Russell to arrive. Janice sat by her side, nervously chewing the inside of her mouth. "He's late," she muttered under her breath.

"He'll be here," replied the detective coolly, pursing her lips in thought.

"Velma, my love," declared a cheery-looking William Russell. He ambled over to the table where they were sat. "And you must be the delectable Janice," he murmured, taking her assistant's hand and kissing it softly. She pulled it away and frowned at the detective, who chuckled throatily.

The detective's eyes twinkled as she said, "It's good to see you, Bill. How was your day?"

"Oh, the usual," he replied, pulling up a seat close to her. "And you, my darling?"

Velma smiled bashfully, "All the better now that you're here, Bill."

He beamed at her and took her hand in his.

"I adore it when you say things like that to me." Janice coughed loudly, interrupting their brief moment of intimacy. "I imagine you want to know if I've any news?" he asked softly. Janice nodded at him pleadingly.

"Well, I've asked around," he replied. "I even spoke with the head of the intelligence services. A rather unpleasant man, I may add. But unfortunately, no one appears to have heard about it. I've asked to be kept informed of any developments, and I'm sure I'll learn something sooner or later. I'm very sorry that it's not better news."

Janice's face fell with disappointment, and the detective squeezed her shoulder sympathetically. "It's still early to be worrying," Velma said, hoping that she sounded more convincing than she actually felt. She was growing increasingly concerned herself at the continued disappearance of Douglas Salter.

"Let me buy you both a drink," offered Russell, feeling a little underwhelmed by the response to his attempts to learn more.

Velma nodded and smiled at him gratefully. "I think brandy is all round on a day like this Bill, if you don't mind?"

He winked at her mischievously, "Right you are, Miss Scott. I'll be back shortly. Perhaps a round of doubles might ease the tension, don't you think?" Grinning at his suggestion, Velma nodded and began sympathetically stroking her assistant's hair.

"I thought you said that he could help," Janice hissed through gritted teeth as Russell disappeared to the bar.

"It's early days Janice, give him a chance."

Her assistant shook her head, "If I don't hear from Douglas by tomorrow, I'm going to call the police, Velma."

The detective sighed and reluctantly nodded her agreement, "All right Janice. Although I doubt it'll help Douglas any."

"Doing nothing won't help him either," retorted her assistant. "Listen, I'm going to head home and leave you to it. I'm tired and it's been a long day…"

"You should stay a while, it's still early Janice." Her assistant shook her head and squeezed Velma's hand. Relenting, Velma squeezed hers back, "I'll see you tomorrow dear, please don't spend all night worrying, we'll find him. I promise."

THIRTY-THREE

Douglas Salter stumbled in his haste and crashed headlong into the waste ground. Wheezing, he doubled over and violently threw up into a hedgerow. He wiped the smear of vomit from his mouth and glanced anxiously over his shoulder. There didn't appear to be anyone tailing him. Despite the protests from his body, he took a few deep breaths and started running again.

After another mile, Douglas finally sagged to the ground, shattered. His heart pounded in his chest, his throat felt dry and brittle. Cautiously, he laid on his back in the long grass of a meadow, hoping it would mask his presence. As nervous exhaustion started to set in, he ruefully stared up at the starlit sky.

The memories of the film footage flickered unrelentingly through his mind like a never-ending horror film. Faces wrought with pain and suffering. He shut his eyes to try and blank them out, but instead, that brought them sharper into focus. Moaning feebly, Douglas tried to focus on something else, anything else. But the images had seared themselves into his mind.

It'll pass eventually, spoke Beatrice's voice soothingly. *You'll never forget what you've seen, but it'll become easier to manage.*

"Beatrice?" croaked Douglas, sitting up and looking around himself with alarm. Somehow, he'd hoped that he'd imagined her voice. A device he'd created to distract himself from the horror of what he'd been forced to watch.

I'm here Douglas, I'm with you now.

The reporter shook his head in an attempt to clear it. *This can't be real,* Douglas told himself firmly. *It must be some sort of delusion, perhaps a mental breakdown?*

I'm afraid not Douglas, intoned the voice in a comforting-sounding lilt. *But as I said, I am here to help you.*

The reporter simply nodded, he was too exhausted to argue, even if it was with himself. Taking a few deep breaths to calm his frayed nerves, he worked up the courage to ask, "How exactly can you help me, Beatrice?"

You started to remember when you saw his face, didn't you? probed the voice. *You recalled something from your past?* Douglas shuddered at the memory. He'd been trying to repress it ever since his escape. *Concentrate on it now. You must remember if you're to understand.*

"I can't," he replied feebly. But it was already too late, and suddenly, images from his childhood swirled through his mind like ephemeral ghosts. Sobbing, Douglas rolled into a ball and clutched his knees to his chest. Clinging on fiercely, his body shuddered involuntarily as one memory after another flooded his mind.

You should rest a while, Beatrice spoke soothingly. *This is going to take time for you to come to terms with.* Douglas didn't

THIRTY-FOUR

Chief Inspector Willis had little time for drunks or vagrants. *This one was wild-eyed, clearly insane,* he thought to himself, as the lurching form of Douglas Salter stumbled against a lamp post. He slowed his car to a crawl beside him and wound down the window. "You there," he bellowed. "I hope you're not planning to cause any trouble. This is a respectable neighbourhood."

Douglas stared at him uncomprehendingly, "Where am I?" he slurred. His clothes were torn, and his face was dirty and covered in scratches and bruises. The Chief Inspector's car screeched to a stop, and the man behind the wheel leapt out.

"I said that I don't want you causing any trouble!" he warned.

Douglas could sense the other man's animosity. It took a moment for him to recognise the police uniform he was wearing. "Please, I need your help," he pleaded. The desperation in his voice caught the Chief Inspector off balance. "I've just escaped from a kidnapping. You have to help me!”

The Chief Inspector sniffed the air between them suspiciously. The man smelt of stale sweat, but he couldn't detect any odour of alcohol. “What's your name?” he asked, relenting slightly.

“Salter, my name's Douglas Salter. I'm a reporter.”

“You're a newspaperman, are you?”

Douglas nodded whilst still clutching tightly to the lamp post. He daren't let go in case he fell down. “I've been drugged,” he replied. “Please, can you help me?” Again, he sensed a change in the other man's attitude towards him. Was it sympathy, pity? Douglas wasn't sure and he didn't really care. Just as long as he'd offer to help.

“Hold out your hands,” ordered the Chief Inspector. Douglas complied and leant his body against the lamppost for support. Grudgingly, the Police Inspector felt the smoothness of the reporter's fingers. “Never done a hard day's work in your life, have you?”

“Well, that depends on your point of view,” argued Douglas meekly, feeling faint.

“Who do you work for?” asked the Chief Inspector, still not entirely convinced, “which newspaper?”

“*The Evening Post*,” replied the reporter, his head swimming. He wasn't sure how, but he could swear that he could hear the thoughts of the policeman questioning him. “I've been a target for some time, and I hired a private investigator to look into my case. You can ask her if you like. She'll vouch for me, her name's Velma Scott.”

The mention of her name appeared to have the desired effect. The Chief Inspector nodded, “Yes, I know of Miss Scott.”

"Just take me to her. She'll explain everything." As Douglas finished speaking, his vision blurred, and he slumped to the ground. The Chief Inspector sighed and looked at his watch. His dinner was going to turn cold, he envisaged the thunderous look on his wife's face when he finally made it home. Tutting to himself, he heaved the prostrate figure of the reporter into the passenger seat of his car and slammed the door shut.

As he started the ignition he turned to glance at his unconscious passenger. "Very well Mr. Salter, we'll see if she's heard of you. Let's hope she'll vouch for your story, otherwise, you'll be spending the night in a cell. That much I can promise you, sir." Douglas Salter didn't reply. Drifting in a sea of blackness, he was tormented by gruesome visions and scarred memories of a forgotten past.

THIRTY-FIVE

Beeton glanced down the bar as he sipped at his beer. A group of regulars hogged the far end, rowdily shooting darts whilst talking and laughing. He didn't notice at first the man taking the bar stool next to him. "Do you mind?" the man asked, tugging gently at Beeton's cuff to draw his attention.

He turned with surprise, "Mind what?" The man gestured at him for a light. Shaking his head, Beeton replied "Sorry, no. I don't smoke."

"Shame," the man said, "you look like you should."

"What does that mean?" Beeton took a moment to study him. The man looked jaded, his clothing equally tired. He appraised the man's features which were craggy and deeply lined. His hair was cropped close to his scalp, but it was his eyes that caught Beeton off guard. Hazel in colour, they appeared youthful and full of vigour in stark contrast to the rest of his features.

"I just meant that you appeared to be the sort of man who enjoyed a smoke. My name's Victor," the man said, introducing himself whilst holding out his hand. "Buy me a drink, and I'll tell you all about myself."

Despite a deeply rooted sense of suspicion, Beeton shrugged, "Why not?" he replied. He had nothing better to do and so he nodded and shook the proffered hand. There was something compelling about the way the man had spoken to him.

"Will a beer suit you, Victor?"

"That's very generous of you, Mr. Beeton."

The intelligence officer stared at him uncertainly, "Have we met before? How'd you know my name?"

"Do you prefer Frank?" countered Victor, avoiding providing him with a straight answer. The barkeep broke the spell as he noisily placed two pints on the bar in front of them.

"Mmm," Beeton muttered distractedly. He slid one of the pints towards Victor, who grinned at him and raised his glass in thanks. "You were saying…" prompted Beeton.

Victor guzzled his drink hungrily, let out a satisfied gasp, and wiped his mouth with the back of his hand. "Yes, that's right, you want to know how I know who you are. Isn't that right?"

Impatiently Beeton tapped the side of his beer glass, he was rapidly losing patience with the other man's procrastination. "You've come here looking for somebody haven't you?" Victor asked, matter-of-factly. "Someone you've been tasked with tracking down by your employer." Shifting uncomfortably in his seat, Beeton stared at him frostily. "Well, you've succeeded. Your search is over, you've found him, Mr. Beeton."

"You?" he responded doubtfully.

Victor nodded and replied, "I'm afraid you've had a wasted trip. Please inform your superior that I'm not interested, I won't be accompanying you to London."

Beeton frowned, "You don't even know what I want, even if you are the person I'm looking for."

"Of course, I do Mr. Beeton," replied Victor calmly. "You want me to help with some research. At least, that's what you've been told by Mr. Cage. Although I doubt that's the entirety of it."

Shocked at the mention of the Defence Chief's name, Beeton rapidly began to reassess the situation he'd found himself in.

"You've been tasked with finding people with certain abilities. One of those people has recently been murdered. I'm not eager to join her, and that is why I'm not volunteering to help. You've gotten yourself embroiled in something that's very dangerous, Mr. Beeton. Something that's far beyond your comprehension and that of your superiors. I suggest that you take the next train home and forget you ever found me."

Unsure how to respond, Beeton chose to remain silent. *How on earth does this man know what I do?* His mind whirred through the gears, as he played out different scenarios. *At least I appear to have found who I'm looking for*, he ruminated. The man facing him adopted an amused look on his face. "This is a matter of urgency," spoke Beeton finally, deciding to appeal to the man's sense of duty.

Victor roared with laughter and clasped him genially around the shoulder, "Mr. Beeton, you are amusing!"

Flushed with annoyance, the intelligence officer shook off Victor's arm and glared at him. "I don't see how?" he muttered. "Neither do I understand how you can possibly know the things you appear to. Unless of course, you have access to information that you shouldn't," he accused suspiciously.

The smile on Victor's face broadened. "If I told you, I'd have to kill you. Isn't that what people say in your trade?" Beeton glanced nervously over his shoulder as Victor spoke. "Don't worry Frank. No one is interested in our conversation, or, who you are."

Beeton hissed, "You're in danger of compromising me and this country."

"I'm doing nothing of the sort," Victor replied calmly. "As I said earlier, the best thing you can do is forget we ever met and take yourself home. I'm certain that Mr. Cage will forgive you in time."

Feeling exasperated, Beeton abruptly stood up. He leant over Victor and prodded him in the chest menacingly. "If I say that your country needs your help, then that is what is required. You don't get to refuse that kind of request."

Unmoved, Victor didn't answer and simply stared at him. Ready to manhandle him if necessary, Beeton stopped suddenly as he caught sight of the man's mesmerising gaze. He was completely unprepared for what happened next.

Beeton saw himself through the other man's eyes. Not just as he was in the present, but in the past and even more disturbingly, in the future. His arms fell limp by his sides as he saw with horror the moment of his own death.

Victor gently guided him back to his barstool and pushed what remained of his warm beer into his shaking hands. "There, there," he said. "Not to worry, it comes for us all Mr. Beeton. It's unavoidable. Now finish your drink and then you'll feel a little better. It's almost time for you to take yourself home."

Robotically, Beeton nodded and finished his drink in one. "I should go," he whispered hoarsely.

Victor nodded, "A very wise choice Frank. The driver who picked you up from the station is waiting outside for you. He'll take you back to the station if you're ready?"

"McLeish?" asked Beeton, barely audibly.

Not unsympathetically, Victor nodded in reply. "Yes, that's right, it's time for you to go."

Paled and horror-stricken, the intelligence officer stumbled out of the pub towards the waiting car and its driver. "Back to London is it, Mr. Beeton?" asked McLeish with a wry smile as he fired up the engine. Wordlessly, Beeton simply nodded. All he knew was that he had to get far away as quickly as possible.

THIRTY-SIX

The Chief Inspector roughly escorted Douglas Salter to the door, propping him against it as he rang the buzzer. "Miss Scott?" he asked over the intercom, "It's Chief Inspector Willis, can I have a word with you, please?"

"What an unexpected pleasure," she trilled. "Do come up dear, I'll buzz you in." The latch on the door opened, and the Chief Inspector took a long, deep breath before he bustled the semi-conscious figure of the reporter up the two flights of steep stairs.

She was already waiting for him. Grunting, he dragged the prostrate figure up the last few steps. "You've found him," she cooed with delight, clapping her hands together. "Well done, Chief Inspector. Mr. Salter has been missing for the last few days and we'd grown rather fond of him. I'm delighted that you've been able to track him down for me. How did you know he was missing?"

Puffing, Chief Inspector Willis rested both himself and the unconscious figure against the wall at the top of the stairwell before replying, "Actually, I didn't, but you're welcome, Miss Scott."

"Is he alright?" asked the detective, concern showing on her face as she noted the reporter's physical condition. Short of breath, Willis simply nodded. "Forgive me, Chief Inspector," she continued. "You must be exhausted, you poor man. If you could just carry him into my office, I'll put the kettle on."

Regretting the moment he'd ever clamped eyes on the reporter, the Chief Inspector sighed and then hauled the figure up to his feet again. Muttering to himself, he dragged the limp form of Douglas Salter through the open door of Velma Scott's office.

"Sugar?" she asked, as he unceremoniously dumped the unconscious figure onto the sofa.

"Please—Miss Scott, would you mind telling me what the devil's going on here? This man, Salter, claimed he'd been kidnapped and drugged!"

"Oh, you've spoken with him? Isn't he delightful? Well, in that case I imagine what he's told you is accurate then," she said, handing the Chief Inspector a steaming hot mug of tea.

"You can't be serious," he exclaimed. He took her silence as confirmation and sighed again. "What have you gotten yourself involved in now?"

"Oh, the usual," she replied with a grin, offering to top off his tea with a dash of brandy. "Skulduggery, espionage, and murder. I suppose I can add kidnapping to the list now you've brought it up."

He shook his head exasperatedly and then let out another sigh. "I think I will have that top-up after all, if you don't mind?"

Beaming, the detective tipped a generous measure of brandy into his mug and invited him to sit down. "Some of this you'll find hard to swallow, Chief Inspector Willis, and I don't mean the tea," she said with a chuckle. Closing his eyes momentarily, he sipped at his drink and waited for the alcohol to take effect. Feeling calmer, he eventually sat down beside her and waited for her to continue.

THIRTY-SEVEN

Janice's hand covered her mouth with shock when she saw the still unstirring form of Douglas Salter the following morning. "Oh my god," she exclaimed loudly, "Douglas!"

Poking her head into the office from the kitchenette and placing her finger to her lips, Velma shushed her, "Quiet—you'll wake him. Although I agree, he does look a little worse for wear, doesn't he? In fact, poor Douglas looks like he's been through a couple of rounds with a prize fighter. Leave him be, I think he could do with the rest."

"But how did he get here? When?" demanded Janice, caressing his face tenderly.

"Late last night," the detective replied. "Chief Inspector Willis discovered him and brought him over here."

"Has he said anything?" asked Janice, noting the scratches and burn marks on his forehead and pointing them out to her employer. Anxiously, the detective's assistant clucked over him, wetting and dabbing her handkerchief as she tried to wipe away the dirt and blood embedded into his face.

Velma nodded at the marks and replied, "Well he hasn't stirred yet. But apparently, Douglas told the Chief Inspector that he'd been kidnapped and drugged just before he passed out."

"Shouldn't we call out a doctor?" the detective's assistant responded, sounding alarmed.

Velma shook her head, "I think he just needs some rest, Janice. Let's wait a while until he comes around. If he needs to see a doctor, we can call one out. Look, I've just put the kettle on, let me make you a drink."

Her assistant folded her arms determinedly, "What if he requires hospital treatment? What if he doesn't wake up?"

Velma Scott's expression softened, as she sought to calm Janice down. "Look, there's no point in getting worked up. He's back now and he's safe, here with us. All we can do is to wait and see for the time being."

The doubt on Janice's face melted slightly, "Alright, Velma, we'll try it your way," she agreed, her voice quavering. "Let's wait and see for now."

Forcing a smile, the detective nodded. "Good girl," she replied. "I think it's the sensible option until we learn what happened to him," she said, doing her best to disguise the alarm in her own voice as she ducked back into the kitchenette. "Tea?" she asked brightly.

"Please," replied Janice, as she tucked the blanket snugly under the reporter's chin. She knelt on the floor beside him and stroked his hair. Blinking back tears, she listened to the tinkle of the spoon stirring the tea in the adjoining room. "Poor you, Douglas," she whispered.

THIRTY-EIGHT

Beeton clasped his hands together nervously as he waited for Harold Cage to finish reading the report he'd submitted. "It's rather brief isn't it?" the Defence Chief remarked when he finally slid the thin folder over to one side on his desk.

"Yes, sir," replied the intelligence officer meekly. "I'm afraid that I didn't have much luck in tracing him down."

"Well, I've had rather more success during your absence."

"Sir?" replied Beeton haltingly, as they were interrupted by a knock on the Defence Chief's office door.

"Come in," barked Cage. He stood up to greet the man who entered and gestured for him to sit down at the far end of the room. "Beeton, this gentleman is here to help us with our little project." The intelligence officer looked over his employer's shoulder towards the tall, thin figure who took the seat pointed out to him by Cage. Well-dressed in a tailored pinstriped suit, the man crossed his long legs and casually glanced in his direction. "This is Mr. Makepeace, Beeton. You're to ensure his comfort and protection at all times. Is that understood?"

The intelligence officer nodded as he studied the waspish face of the figure at the far end of the room. There was something about the amused look on his face that made him feel distinctly uncomfortable. Beeton stood up and wandered over towards the spindly figure. "It's a pleasure to make your acquaintance, sir." Limply, the man shook his hand, seemingly indifferent to their meeting.

"Mr. Makepeace has lodgings at the Ritz, Beeton. You're required to stand guard outside his room during the evenings and to accompany him during his visits to us in the day. You'll be relieved at midnight, but I expect you to be back outside his room by six-thirty each morning."

The intelligence officer nodded affirmatively and replied, "Yes, sir."

"Very well," continued Cage. "Mr. Makepeace, it's a pleasure as always. If you have any additional requirements, please make them known to Beeton, here. I'm sure he'll endeavour to meet your requests." The man half-smiled, displaying a row of discoloured teeth, and nodded as he rose from his chair. "Please escort our guest back to his suite, Mr. Beeton."

The intelligence officer watched as the man shook hands with the Defence Chief. Suddenly the figure loomed over him, "Come on Mr. Beeton, I don't want to waste any more of Mr. Cage's precious time. It's prudent not to dawdle, don't you think?"

Tight-lipped, the intelligence officer simply nodded and held open the office door. "After you, Mr. Makepeace," he eventually replied as the figure swept through ahead of him. He watched as the man hurriedly disappeared up the steps at the end of the corridor and shuddered. *Working with that man's going to be painful*, he mused.

THIRTY-NINE

The unsubtle aroma of over-stewed coffee stirred Douglas Salter from his stupor. He stretched and forced his eyes open, taking in his surroundings. "Douglas—you're awake at last!" trilled a familiar voice. "That is a relief, how are you feeling?"

"Miss Scott," the reporter croaked with surprise, his voice gravelly. "What are you doing here? In fact, where am I and how did I get here?"

"You're safe and sound, Douglas. You're in my office and recovering on my sofa once again." Chuckling she said, "At this rate I'm going to have to start charging you rent." He groaned in reply and rolled over onto his side. Velma shoved a mug under his nose and urged him to get up, "I want to check that you're alright."

He reluctantly nodded and swung his feet onto the wooden floor. As soon as he was upright, his head began to swim. "I feel terrible," he muttered, fighting the urge to vomit. The detective fussed over him, focusing on the burns, cuts, and bruises whilst tutting loudly. "Well?" he asked eventually, "Do you think I'll live?"

She chastised him gently, "Sarcasm is the preserve of the uneducated Douglas. I expect better from you." He nodded apologetically and regretted it instantly as the bile rose at the back of his throat. Noting the sudden change in his complexion, she hurriedly shoved the waste bin under his nose. "Don't hold back on my account, Douglas, just let it all out." He didn't stop to answer, he was too busy heaving up his guts.

Velma hurried into the kitchen whilst the wave of nausea passed over the reporter. When she returned, the detective gently dabbed at his forehead with a cold, damp cloth. "Get some rest, Douglas. We'll talk again when you're feeling better."

Unable to speak as the room spun violently, he nodded and leant against the plump cushions on the sofa. As the reporter's eyes closed, the din of voices in his mind slowly subsided. Gratefully, he let out a sigh and sank into a troubled sleep.

Protectively, the detective watched over him, the concern etched into her forehead. She sensed that something was wrong, but until Douglas was able to explain what had happened, she didn't know what to do. Her brow furrowed as he mumbled something in his sleep, "make peace" he repeated softly, over and over. Velma shook her head, it would have to keep until he was well enough to talk.

FORTY

In the dim light of the grey, overcast morning, Beeton ignored the patter of rain and the complaints of the man under his protection. "Why can't we take a car?" asked Makepeace for the third time in as many minutes. "I don't think you realise how precarious my situation is."

"Mr. Makepeace, it'll take twice as long if we drive, the traffic's murder this time of day. Besides, it's only a short trip, and I'll have you there in no time. You're quite safe with me. I have two men up ahead of us and another behind. No one is going to harm you whilst you're in my care."

The spindly figure scowled, "I doubt Mr. Cage would be happy with your choices. You're supposed to guarantee my safety. Is he aware of this travel decision? Or is this something of your own devising, Mr. Beeton?"

"We're only five minutes away, Mr. Makepeace. Let me assure you that this is the quickest route."

Stooping so that he was face-to-face with the intelligence officer protecting him, Makepeace stopped abruptly in the street and hissed, "If we're so safe, why is someone following us, Mr. Beeton?"

The intelligence officer shook his head exasperatedly, "Look, I'd know if someone were following. One of my men would have spotted him by now."

"Hah," snorted Makepeace derisively, unconvinced by his escort's reassurances. He turned and stared suspiciously at a man in a heavy-looking overcoat and then glared at Beeton. "I imagine that they're about ready to intercede." Anxiously looking back over his shoulder, Makepeace muttered, "That man's a Soviet agent. Beware his concealed weapon, it's hidden in his shoe."

Disbelievingly, Beeton turned to look at the man Makepeace had pointed out. He was unremarkable-looking, overweight, and balding. The man paused to close his umbrella as the drizzle slowed. As Beeton searched the throng of people behind them for the officer, he'd posted up to watch their backs, the man Makepeace suspected of being a Soviet agent, veered suddenly in their direction.

Worryingly, the officer who Frank Beeton had instructed to watch over them was nowhere to be seen. He felt inside his pocket for the reassuring grip of his revolver and hurriedly studied the gait of the approaching figure. "Stay behind me," Beeton barked, placing himself in front of Makepeace. "If something happens and you need to run, don't think twice, understand?" He didn't have time to listen for a reply as at that moment, the figure struck.

Beeton batted away the umbrella that swung towards him and stepped up close to his assailant. His hand reached towards the man's throat as he strove to defend both himself and the man in his charge.

The figure growled something and Beeton jumped back as a gleam of metal suddenly swished by his ear. He caught the man's outstretched foot mid-air and twisted it. As he swerved to avoid the protruding blade at the tip of his attacker's shoe, Beeton ignored the blows that rained down upon him. Twisting this way and that, he wrestled the shoe from his attacker and shoved him to the ground.

The intelligence officer smiled grimly as the assailant glared at him. Beeton let the man's shoe drop to the floor as he prepared to take him. He was unprepared for the blow that caught him from behind. Staggering, he fell to his knees as another blow smashed into his skull. His vision blurring, Beeton could only watch with dismay as the one-shoed attacker suddenly leapt to his feet and scuttled away into the crowd.

Groaning, the dazed intelligence officer twisted around to look behind him. But whoever had attacked him had vanished as well. As he climbed to his feet, he desperately sought the man in his charge—Makepeace. But there was no sign of him. Praying that he'd run as instructed, Beeton gathered up the assailant's shoe and headed for the office. Cage wouldn't be happy, the intelligence officer realised, as he hurried miserably towards where he hoped Makepeace was now holed up.

***

Cage growled menacingly as he spied Beeton entering the atrium of the office building without his charge. "Where's Makepeace?" he barked from the top of the stairwell.

"There was an incident, sir," the intelligence officer replied, hurriedly starting up the stairwell. "I'd hoped he'd made it back here already. I just came over in order to check."

"You hoped…" exclaimed the Defence Chief belligerently from the top of the stairwell, balling his fist tightly. "My office—now," growled the Defence Chief. Forlornly, Beeton complied and trudged up the marble staircase towards his boss, whose face had turned crimson. He did his best to ignore the wry smiles of colleagues as they passed him and he edged towards his boss. A thick file of paper unexpectedly caught Beeton across the back of the head, "That's for embarrassing me."

Beeton flinched as Cage whacked him across the back of the head again with his file, "And that's for embarrassing the department. You want another for embarrassing yourself?" he threatened.

Meekly Beeton shook his head. Cage irritably shoved Beeton, down the corridor towards his office. "You'll be lucky if you're not up on charges after this" he snarled, "How many bouts of ineptitude do you think you can get away with?"

Tight-lipped, the intelligence officer pushed open Cage's door and let out a sigh of relief as he spied Makepeace in an armchair opposite the Defence Chief's desk. "You're here?" he remarked incredulously.

"Of course, I'm here," replied Makepeace. "Where else would I be?"

Cage shoved Beeton aside, "Are you sure that you're alright, Mr. Makepeace?" he asked, shooting a venomous look at the intelligence officer beside him.

He smiled graciously, "Yes, of course, Mr. Cage. It's good of you to inquire."

Hurrying towards his desk, Cage poured two large brandies. "I heard that an incident had taken place?" he said, offering one to Makepeace and sipping at the other himself.

Makepeace nodded, "Luckily your man here, Beeton, intervened on my behalf. I don't know what I would have done otherwise. I was lucky he was there to protect me." Cage eyeballed Beeton waspishly as he gestured for Makepeace to sit back down.

"Wait outside Beeton, it looks like it's your lucky day," he ordered, dismissing the intelligence officer offhand. Furiously, Beeton looked from Cage to Makepeace and then strode outside, slamming the door shut after him.

Topping up his guest's drink, Cage leant back in his chair. "Let me apologise for his attitude," Cage added earnestly. "It's very difficult to get hold of good staff these days."

Makepeace dismissed his apology with a nonchalant flick of the wrist. "Shall we get down to business, Mr. Cage? I'm eager to resume our work on your little project."

"As am I Mr. Makepeace—as am I."

FORTY-ONE

A thick carpet of fog cascaded over the river bank and crept across the deserted cobbled footpath. Undulating as it swirled around the street lights, the blanket of mist sank and settled over the street. Despite the gloom, Douglas hurried towards the wrought iron bridge that crossed the river. Skeleton-like, its form emerged like a prehistoric beast as he drew closer. A sense of unease followed him, and he pulled the collar of his coat up around his neck.

The luminous full moon cast an eerie and otherworldly glow over the rush of water below. And despite the incessant rainfall, the swollen banks of the river stubbornly flowed, seemingly undeterred. Frothing as the water surged through a bottleneck, the current urged the mangled remains of a bloated corpse downstream. Face down, the body bobbed and weaved as it coursed through the swell.

The body didn't immediately register with the reporter, a fleeting glimpse of a familiar shape which passed beneath him on the bridge. Douglas stopped and waited for a break in the mist as he stared over the side into the darkness. A shock of recognition suddenly passed over his face. The shape he'd noticed belonged to a checkered shirt, and he gasped as he caught sight of a body, intertwined within it, which drifted helplessly past.

Unsure of what to do, Douglas hurtled towards the far end of the bridge. But by the time he'd reached the other side, he was already too late. Lost in the murky depths, the body had seemingly vanished.

Urgently, he jumped down the embankment, scanning the river. The corpse had gotten itself lodged in the thick bramble that lined the near side of the river bank. Ignoring the brambles and the stench of decay, he reached towards it, grimacing. The skin felt cold to the touch as it brushed against his hand, closing his eyes, Douglas heaved it onto the bank.

As he rolled the body over, the face appeared bloated and pockmarked. Douglas covered his mouth and nose with one hand as he searched for the man's wallet and some form of identification with the other.

At that very moment, he heard a shout somewhere above him, followed by a shrill whistle. It slowly dawned on Douglas how it looked, his leaning over a dead body as a local bobby pointed at him and ordered him to stay where he was. Nodding, the reporter backed away from the corpse and raised his hands.

"I just found him," he yelled. "I saw him from the bridge." The policeman shoved him aside as he leant over the corpse.

"You can explain yourself at the station," he

muttered, giving the reporter a suspicious look. "Don't you dare move." He blew repeatedly on his whistle until three more policemen joined them on the river bank. "Take him in for questioning, will you," ordered the policeman who'd initially spotted Douglas. "And get a car down here, pronto. We'll likely need an autopsy to establish the cause of death." His colleague nodded as he slipped a pair of cuffs around Douglas's wrists.

"You don't need those. I'll come with you willingly," protested Douglas.

"Too right you will," agreed the policeman, shoving him back up the embankment. "Don't think I wouldn't enjoy giving you a good hiding. I've no time for liars and murderers."

"What the hell are you talking about?" Douglas argued. "Look at the state of him. It's obvious that the body has been in the water for a while. It's all bloated."

The policeman took a cursory glance at the corpse, he was missing a shoe on one foot. "We'll see about that," growled the policeman, giving the reporter another shove. "I'll have a car with you shortly," he announced to his colleagues. Sullenly, Douglas was frogmarched to the nearby police station. It didn't matter what he said, the arresting officer was convinced of his guilt or at least of his involvement. Shaking his head wearily, Douglas clammed up and instead said nothing. "Your silence won't help you," muttered the policeman. Douglas looked away; it was pointless to argue with him, he could sense it.

***

Chief Inspector Willis rolled his eyes despairingly as he looked in on the reporter, holed up in the cell. "Has he said anything yet?"

The arresting officer shook his head. "Not really, sir. He was found at the scene and protested his innocence of course. We're waiting on a report from the pathologist before we interrogate him."

"I'll have a word with him," sighed Willis. "I know this man." The policeman looked at the Chief Inspector questioningly but said nothing. Instead, he simply nodded and fetched the keys to the cell. "Would you give Velma Scott a call for me?" asked the Chief Inspector. His colleague nodded and ambled back towards the desk.

A hatch in the cell door slammed shut, and the rustle of keys in the lock sounded. Douglas looked up from the cell bunk forlornly, and then let out a sigh of relief as he recognised the Chief Inspector. "I'm so glad it's you," he admitted.

"Don't get your hopes up too soon, Mr. Salter. In my experience, people only come to my attention this frequently when they've done something wrong."

The reporter sighed, "I found the body, that's all. I've no involvement whatsoever." He studied the Chief Inspector's face closely, watching for a response.

"I don't doubt that," Willis finally admitted after a lengthy silence. "Still, you can't deny that these things start to stack up after a while."

"I was just in the wrong place at the wrong time," Douglas admitted. "I've been unlucky, that's all."

"Well, that's one way of looking at it I suppose. Listen, I've asked one of the officers to call Miss Scott for you," the Chief Inspector replied. "Once the pathologist confirms how long the body has been in the water for, I don't imagine we'll keep you too long." Douglas nodded with relief. "Tell me, is there any connection between the body and your alleged kidnapping, Mr. Salter?"

"None that I'm aware of," replied Douglas. "As I said, I've just been unlucky recently."

"Well, I'd suggest that you don't make a habit of it," replied Willis. "You're fortunate I was even down here tonight. Otherwise, you'd likely be in here all night."

"Perhaps my luck is changing," ventured the reporter.

"Perhaps," agreed the Chief Inspector. "I'll have someone bring you in a cup of tea."

"I could do with something stronger," Douglas muttered. Willis ignored him. "Once Miss Scott arrives, I'll release you into her custody until this matter is resolved. Now try and stay out of trouble in the meantime, won't you."

"I'll certainly try, Chief Inspector," agreed the reporter, determined to do that very thing. Satisfied with the response, Willis shut the cell door and retreated down the corridor. Douglas let out a deep sigh, swung his legs back onto the cot, and closed his eyes.

FORTY-TWO

The echo of footsteps approached outside the cell door. Obscene graffiti daubed the walls and the cell stank of stale urine. Optimistically, Douglas opened his eyes, he was eager to leave. As the key turned in the lock, his heart sank. It wasn't the detective, and neither was it the Chief Inspector. A tall, callow-skinned figure leered at him. "Douglas, how wonderful to see you again."

The reporter's heart raced as he tried to quell his rising sense of fear, "Makepeace," he spat.

The man grinned menacingly, "I see that it's all starting to come back to you. Well, that's excellent news. I'm eager to renew our acquaintance."

Douglas glanced anxiously over the man's shoulder, "How'd you even get in here?"

"Access, my dear boy. It's all about access. As you can see, I have it, and you don't." They studied one another for a moment, sizing each other up. "I think it's time we had a little chat, don't you?" Douglas glared at him furiously. "Temper, temper," chided Makepeace. "That attitude will only make things more difficult for you in the long run."

"I've no idea what you're talking about," growled the reporter. "But any second now, the Chief Inspector will be in here to let me out. I imagine he'd enjoy a long talk with you."

Makepeace giggled, he sounded almost childlike. "I very much doubt that, my dear Douglas. You see, we have something in common: you and I. But the difference is, you're only just coming to terms with your gift, whilst I have honed mine over decades. When we first met Douglas, you used to refer to me as your master. Are you willing to re-establish our prior relationship and continue your education with me?"

A snarl spread across the reporter's face. "There's nothing you can teach me," hissed Douglas, drawing his knees defensively up against his chest.

Makepeace grinned maliciously, "I see that you remember more than you care to let on." Ignoring his pointed remark, Douglas sprang up from the cot and dove aggressively towards him. Laughing, Makepeace stood his ground as Douglas suddenly froze, unable to move. Enjoying the moment, Makepeace slowly circled around him. "Are you quite sure there's nothing I can teach you, Douglas?"

Sweat broke out across the reporter's forehead as he struggled to will his body to respond. He was close to panic as Makepeace made his way around the reporter's prostrate body, chuckling. "I'll kill you," Douglas managed to growl.

Makepeace stopped laughing and adopted a serious look, "I suspect your intentions are true, Douglas, even if the likelihood of you achieving your goal is rather doubtful to say the least." Enjoying the minutiae of the moment, he ruffled the reporter's hair fondly. "The offer still stands, Douglas. Why don't you come and work with me? I'll teach you how to use the gift I've bestowed on you."

Grunting from the effort, Douglas managed to turn his head so that he was face-to-face with his assailant. Makepeace smiled proudly. "Well done, boy. You're a lot stronger at this stage of your development than I ever was. I always suspected that you had a natural aptitude for this. Why don't you join me? So we can realise the full extent of your abilities, together."

Spittle flew from Douglas's mouth like a projectile, catching Makepeace square in the face. Douglas wasn't sure who was more surprised, himself or the spindly figure standing opposite him. Makepeace wiped away the phlegm with a gloved hand and studied it with interest. "This is your last chance, Douglas," he said in a low voice. "I'd grab this opportunity if I were you. After this, things will only become more unpleasant." The reporter tried to spit in Makepeace's direction again, but the figure from his past somehow maintained a vice-like grip over him. "Very well," snarled Makepeace, "you always were a stubborn boy."

Douglas sank to his knees as if a huge weight suddenly bared down upon him. He felt a steady pressure encroaching around his throat. Makepeace watched on impassively, as the reporter struggled for breath. "Only now do you realise the extent of the power I was willing to share with you, now when it's too late." Douglas gurgled, his hands clasping around his own neck as he fought for every breath.

The unexpected sound of voices outside the cell caused Makepeace to frown. He released his mental grip and hurried out into the corridor. Choking, Douglas collapsed to the ground, urgently gulping down air. His cell door swung open again, and the Chief Inspector entered. He rushed to the reporter's assistance. "Call a doctor!" he bellowed, loosening Douglas's tie and collar.

"He's out there," gasped Douglas, his hand shaking as he pointed towards the door.

Chief Inspector Willis helped him up onto the cot. "There's no one out there, Mr. Salter. This place has a single point of entry, and no one has gotten past me."

"He was here," insisted Douglas, his hand bawling into a fist. "Makepeace was here." The reporter's breaths grew shallow as his eyes rolled back into their sockets, and he passed out.

FORTY-THREE

elma sat beside the reporter on the cot in his cell, watching over him with a concerned expression on his face. "Have you seen the bruises around his throat?" she asked, looking pointedly at Chief Inspector Willis. "Are you absolutely positive that no one else has been in here with him?"

Mystified, Willis shook his head, "I don't see how. I'd have seen them if that were the case, Miss Scott."

"Then how do you explain these?" persisted the detective. The Chief Inspector shrugged helplessly as the reporter began to stir. "Douglas?"

His eyes opened slowly, "Miss Scott," the reporter croaked, his voice sounding harsh as he sat up. "When did you get here?"

"I've been here a while," she replied, standing up and shooing the Chief Inspector outside. "I hear that there's been a bit of trouble?"

"Makepeace was here, in this cell," muttered Douglas darkly. "He said that he had access, and from what I can make out, he appears to be able to come and go as he pleases."

She nodded, "The Chief Inspector mentioned that you'd thought someone had been in here with you. But he insisted that no one passed him outside in the corridor. Tell me Douglas, who is this Makepeace character?"

Douglas shook his head, "I know what I saw Miss Scott. And I know what happened in this cell. Do you think that I can get out of here now?"

She smiled sympathetically, "I'm concerned for you Douglas. You've bruises around your throat, and I'm not convinced you've fully recovered from your kidnapping. Trauma can affect people in unexpected ways. I'd like you to come see a friend of mine, he's a doctor."

"I'm fine," snapped the reporter irritably. "I know who and what I saw. I'm not making it up, Miss Scott. Makepeace wanted me to come and work with him, but I turned down his offer. I'd never help that vile son of a bitch."

Concern etched over her face. She asked, "And the bruises around your neck?"

"He did that when I refused his offer," replied Douglas softly. "If Chief Inspector Willis hadn't interrupted him, I doubt that we'd be having this conversation now." She peered at him curiously, "I know how it sounds," he admitted, bowing his head. "But it's no less strange than anything else that's been happening recently. The funny thing is, he did all this without even laying a finger on me. I just don't understand how."

Velma squeezed his shoulder comfortingly.

"I wanted to hit him, Miss Scott, but I just couldn't

move. I was utterly powerless in his presence, frozen still, like a statue." Douglas sighed wearily, "I got the impression that he was just toying with me. That he could have finished me whenever he wanted. It was terrifying."

At a loss, Velma shook her head. Douglas seemed confused and, more worryingly, resigned to his fate. Covered in bruises and welts, he trembled with anxiety as she reached out to him. "Douglas, I don't know what to say, my dear."

His face paled and he recoiled from her touch as the memory played back in his mind. Attempting to compose himself, he asked, "What's happened with the body I found by the river, am I free to leave yet?"

Velma took his arm and helped him to his feet. She replied, "That's another unexpected twist. The body had no identification on it whatsoever. But the pathologist found a couple of faded tattoos on the victim's left arm. The lettering was Cyrillic, Russian of all things." She shook her head with bewilderment, "I really don't understand the connection at this point. Let's go and get a drink Douglas, it's been a tough day all around. This one's on me."

Gratefully, the reporter smiled at her, "Thanks, Velma, I could really do with one right now. In fact, I could do with quite a few more than one."

Grinning easily, she replied, "I imagined that'd be the case." The detective rapped sharply on the cell door, "My client and I are leaving now," she announced to the Chief Inspector, still waiting outside the cell. "Open up please, Mr. Willis."

***

Curious as to the nature of their relationship, Makepeace watched with interest as Miss Scott and the reporter left the supposed sanctity of the police station. "She's rather interesting," he muttered to himself, tapping his driver on the shoulder. "Let's go," he commanded. The car slowly pulled away from the curb and Makepeace settled himself comfortably into the back seat. "Miss Velma Scott," he murmured under his breath, already starting to plan his next move.

FORTY-FOUR

Beeton waited impassively outside of the Defence Chief's office. Behind closed doors, Cage and Makepeace clinked glasses before throwing back their respective drinks. "A top-up?" asked Cage generously, holding out a hand for his new colleague's empty glass. Makepeace nodded and yawned as he settled back into the leather armchair by the fireplace. "So, you mentioned that you'd come across a prospective test subject?" mentioned Cage casually, suppressing his natural urge to demand all the information at once.

Makepeace nodded thoughtfully and took a long sip of his drink. "Yes, that's right Mr. Cage. He has a strong natural ability, untrained, of course." The Defence Chief nodded expectantly. "He's a newspaperman by trade," continued Makepeace, "you know the sort, deals in tittle-tattle. To get him onside, I suspect that we'll need to find just the right lever in order to motivate him."

"Carrot or stick?" asked Cage, grinning unpleasantly.

"Oh, definitely a stick," chuckled Makepeace, returning Cage's malicious grin. "He's far too moralistic to help for any other reason."

The Defence Chief nodded his understanding, "I see, one of those lefties is he?"

Makepeace shrugged his shoulders, "He is what he is, Mr. Cage. Unfortunately, that aspect of his personality is quite beyond our control."

"And does this man have a name?" asked Cage curiously.

Makepeace chuckled softly, "Salter," he replied. "His name is Douglas Salter." A brief flicker of recognition passed over the Defence Chief's face at the mention of the name. "Do you know of him?" enquired Makepeace.

The Defence Chief shook his head, "No, never heard of the man."

The spindly figure sat opposite him nodded craftily and then raised his glass, "Well in that case, to the project, Mr. Cage." They toasted with another clink of glass as Makepeace began to casually trawl through the Defence Chief's memories. It didn't take him long before he settled on a name, William Russell, the government's Chief Science Advisor. He smiled graciously at his host, "I think it's time I met with our Chief Science Advisor, don't you agree Mr. Cage?"

The Defence Chief nodded with surprise at the mention of his colleague. "I don't see why not, now that you've identified a viable subject for our project."

Makepeace smiled disarmingly, "Would you mind if that happened today?"

Cage nodded, mistaking his new colleague's

eagerness for efficiency. "Yes of course, I'll have Beeton escort you over to his office if you'd like?"

Satisfied with the outcome of their conversation, Makepeace sank into the soft, comfortable chair, soaking up the warm glow emanating from the fireplace. "That'll be perfect Mr. Cage, absolutely perfect."

***

Beeton escorted the tall, pinstriped figure to the offices of William Russell. The stripes served to make his charge seem even more slender than he actually was. They also seemed to make him appear taller. He already cut an imposing figure and towered over the intelligence officer beside him.

The man's looming gait and near-skeletal appearance made Beeton feel uncomfortable. He deliberately stared straight ahead and avoided looking over at the visitor. As they rounded the maze of corridors in silence, he thought he heard a soft chuckle from the man beside him. Unable to resist the urge, he looked up.

Predator-like, the man's mesmerising gaze locked on him. Drawn hypnotically in, the intelligence officer's skin crawled as they slowed their pace. They stopped abruptly at the end of a long corridor and Beeton shivered, despite himself.

In that single moment of eye contact, Beeton understood all that he needed. His presence was tolerated, for the time being. He nodded his compliance, and the man adopted a sinister smile on his paper-thin lips.

Regretting it instantly, the intelligence officer took

a deep breath. The appearance of the Defence Chief's mysterious and intimidating visitor hadn't improved matters. If it was even possible, things now appeared even worse.

Launching into a hurried stride, Beeton escorted his guest towards the three polished oak doors which lay ahead. "He mightn't be immediately available," he muttered aloud, "but his secretary will know of his immediate whereabouts."

Dwelling for more than a moment that was necessary, Beeton felt the man's eyes burrowing into his skull. He understood that his use as a necessary guide through the labyrinth of offices was no longer needed and his continuing presence deemed unimportant.

Disregarded, Beeton warily stole another glance as he knocked with authority on the door in front of them. He caught his breath as he glimpsed a distorted vision of himself through the older man's eyes. The disfigured reflection stared back at him, unblinking. Crippled by anxiety, Beeton rapidly grew aware that he was sweating profusely. Even Cage, his boss, hadn't ever managed to rattle him to this extent.

He ground his teeth uneasily whilst they waited. Anxiety gnawed at him in the presence of an individual who radiated a power that seemingly enabled him to compel others to do his bidding. For them to wordlessly obey...it made Beeton feel as though he was a child in the company of a much older, wiser adult. He'd never admit it publicly, but this particular individual was one of the most terrifying people he'd ever encountered.

"Do you know Mr. Russell well?" enquired

Makepeace casually.

Beeton remained steadfast as he waited beside him for an imminent reply to his knock on the door. Hesitantly, he replied, "Not really, sir."

Makepeace nodded, noting the fact Beeton's mind strayed towards a supposed dalliance between Russell and the detective, Scott. "That's very interesting," he mused.

Curious, suspicious, and frightened in equal measure, Beeton ignored his initial impulse and replied noncommittally, "If you say so, sir." To his relief, the Chief Science Advisor's secretary finally opened the office door. "Is Mr. Russell available?" demanded the intelligence officer, sounding close to desperation.

Sandra, his secretary, shook her head. "Sorry, he's finished a little early today. Although, I dare say that you might be able to still catch him, if you hurry. Mr. Russell left ten minutes ago."

Nodding his thanks, Beeton looked apprehensively at the figure beside him. "What do you want to do, Mr. Makepeace?"

"Let's attempt to catch up with him. He may not know it yet, but Mr. Russell could very well be in possession of knowledge that's vital to the success of our project."

"I know you can't tell me the ins and outs, sir, but what exactly does this project entail?

Adopting an expression of surprise, Makepeace replied, "What, you don't know? Well, well, Mr. Beeton…, I appreciate and understand why governments prefer to keep their dirty little secrets to themselves. Nonetheless, some information has to be shared in order to achieve success. How can you be expected to serve to the best of your ability if you know nothing of what we're working towards?"

Beeton shrugged with an adopted air of indifference, "It's just the nature of the job, sir."

Makepeace replied, "I'll fill you in whilst we walk if you like."

The intelligence officer normally leapt at opportunities like this. But this was different and much more dangerous. Finally, he nodded and said, "I know of a pub or two on Russell's route home. He stops in occasionally. I think our best bet is to try one of those first."

Makepeace smiled humourlessly, "I trust your instincts regarding this matter, Mr. Beeton. Why don't you escort me?"

The intelligence officer nodded uncertainly. Undoubtedly, this information would come with a price tag attached. He just didn't know what it was yet. "I am at your disposal, Mr. Makepeace. Might I suggest that if you could somehow assist me, sir, we could track him down together much faster."

Sanguinely, the spindly figure replied, "It doesn't work like that I'm afraid. But I think you'll be surprised at what I have to tell you, perhaps even a little astonished."

The intelligence officer's mind raced with possibilities. He was well used to dealing with the inflated egos of those who kept secrets. But this situation was entirely different.

Is it the price it carries that's making you hesitant? Makepeace asked him wordlessly.

Overcome with curiosity, Beeton couldn't resist his overtures; he knew that he had to learn more. Drawn in, he chose to disregard the inherent threat posed to his own well-being. Instead, he simply nodded and listened intently as Makepeace whispered in his mind. Possessors of this power, like the one which Makepeace was employing right now, had learnt to use something that was reverently referred to as: *The Knowledge*.

Beeton shook his head in confusion, was he imagining all this? He couldn't understand how it was possible. *I know you don't*, sounded Makepeace wordlessly. *It's just something that you'll have to learn to accept. This is the way of the future, this is how wars will be won and lost. This is why Harold Cage is so desperate to have it first.*

Makepeace clicked his fingers, and the spell was suddenly broken. Startled, Beeton looked about himself with surprise, they were already outside in the open air. "How?" he asked incredulously. But Makepeace was already ten steps ahead of him and veering through the crowded streets. Beeton raced after him like a lovesick puppy, eager to please his new master.

FORTY-FIVE

William Russell sighed contentedly and wiped the froth from his mouth with the back of his hand. He gestured to the barman for a refill and checked the time on his wristwatch, which read five forty-five.

"Cooey," exclaimed Velma, waving excitedly as she spotted him at the bar.

Grinning like a love-struck schoolboy, he beckoned her over eagerly. "Velma, my dear, can I get you a drink?"

"Oh, just the usual for me please, Bill." They gazed at each other adoringly as the barman saw to their order, and tenderly, they wove their fingers through each other's. Wordlessly, as they held hands, the couple made their way over towards a deserted table in the corner of the pub.

"How's your friend, Mr. Salter, getting along?" asked Russell pleasantly, breaking the spell between them. The detective shook her head and sighed as she reached for her drink. "I see," mumbled Russell. "Anything I can do to help?"

Velma shook her head again, "I doubt it, Bill. Not unless you happen to know something about telepathy?" She laughed, hearing how odd it must have sounded as she said it aloud.

As her words registered, the Science Chief's face fell. "Velma, what exactly do you mean by that?"

"It's nothing," she said, trying to brush her comment aside. "Forget I ever said anything, I was being indiscreet, and it's terribly unprofessional of me."

Absently caressing his pint glass, Russell replied, "I'd really like to hear more. Please, Velma, it might be important," he persisted, his curiosity piqued.

"I can't Bill," protested the detective. "Please don't ask me again." A long silence descended between them, and they sat looking at each other over the table.

Hesitantly, Russell finally spoke up, "I actually do know a bit about telepathy you know." A little shocked by his admission, she waited for him to continue. "You see, I've been involved in a project at work…it's all hush, hush you understand?" The detective nodded apprehensively, wondering where he was going with this. "I really can't say much, but suffice it to say, that telepathy is actually a real phenomenon."

He'd thought that she'd be surprised by his admission, but instead, she whispered, "I already know that Bill."

It was his turn to be surprised. "Are you saying that your client has displayed certain abilities, Velma? Perhaps even something approaching telepathy?"

Reluctantly she nodded, "What's more Bill, he doesn't appear to be the only one."

"You know of others?" Russell asked incredulously.

"I know of at least one more, or at least my client, Mr. Salter, does. He says that the other man he's come into contact with is far more powerful. That this man somehow has the means to prevent anyone from physically moving. That he comes and goes as he pleases, does whatever he likes, without fear of reprisals."

"That's a rather extraordinary claim," remarked Russell, adopting a doubtful expression. "Do you believe him, Velma?"

Smiling sadly, Velma squeezed Bill's hand tightly and nodded. "It's not often I say this, but at this moment in time, I'm not sure what I can actually do to help my client." A melancholy silence descended over the table once again. Sitting across from each other, both lost in their own private worlds, their thoughts turned to the reporter, Douglas Salter.

***

"Extraordinary," remarked Makepeace, as he watched from the far end of the pub. "It's almost as extraordinary as your lack of surprise as to the nature of this project, Mr. Beeton."

"I told you already, Mr. Makepeace, it takes a lot to surprise me."

"I'd have thought the idea of telepathy would certainly have caused you some consternation though," remarked Makepeace, distractedly.

Beeton smirked, mistaking Makepeace's words for concern as to the nature of their evolving relationship.

"They've been cosying up for a while now," confirmed the intelligence officer, nodding towards the detective and the Chief Science Advisor. "I've reported their dalliance to Mr. Cage of course."

Nodding distractedly, Makepeace replied, "I'm sure you have Mr. Beeton." Curiously, he began to scan the minds of the couple as they tentatively stroked each other's hands.

FORTY-SIX

The train pulled slowly into Euston station, steam wafting over the bulbous engine as the screeching of brakes brought it to a bone-shuddering stop. Whilst the passengers disembarked, a somewhat dishevelled-looking figure joined them on the platform. He whistled loudly as he took in the grandeur of the station. Craggy-faced, the man grinned impishly and set off towards the exit.

He came to a halt outside, the sea of people on the busy street catching him by surprise. Recoiling from the throng, he muttered, "So this is how London looks now," as he spied the tower of University College Hospital opposite the entrance to the train station. He took a moment to gather his wits and then hailed a passing taxi cab. "Mayfair, if you please, driver," he said in a thick Scottish accent.

The cab driver looked dubiously at his passengers' tired and worn clothing, and shrugged; it was none of his business. "Right you are, gov."

***

Douglas was enjoying a luxurious afternoon tea with Janice at Claridges. They'd gorged themselves on salmon and cucumber sandwiches, and were enjoying a generous helping of scones and tea. "I do love the weekends," remarked Janice as she bit into another cream topped scone.

"Me too," mumbled Douglas, a half-stuffed scone already in his mouth leaving a thick smear of jam across his chin. Janice gazed fondly at him as she dabbed at the mess with a serviette. Sheepishly, Douglas smiled back at her tenderly. The look on the reporter's face fell suddenly as he spied a dishevelled figure approaching their table.

"What is it?" asked Janice, noting the apprehensive expression on Douglas's face.

"I'm not sure yet," he replied, gently ushering her hand away from his chin and wiping at his mouth with a serviette. "Let me handle this."

"Douglas Salter?" asked the man in a thick Scottish brogue as he pulled up a chair. The reporter nodded. "My apologies for interrupting your lunch, but I must speak with you."

Douglas raised an eyebrow quizzically in response, "About what exactly? Who are you?"

The Scott, Victor, looked hesitantly over at Janice. "I trust her implicitly," insisted Douglas.

"Very well—Mr. Salter. I was recently paid a visit by one of Her Majesty's intelligence operatives, a Mr. Beeton." Douglas scowled at the mention of the name. Victor smiled knowingly, "I see you've met him already?"

Nodding, the reporter replied, "Yes, he has an unfortunate tendency to turn up in places where he's not welcome. Recently, he's more often than not in the exact same places I am. And, if I'm being completely honest." Douglas looked around the room suspiciously as if half expecting to see the agent suddenly appear in their midst at the mere mention of his name. "I'm a little surprised he isn't here right now."

Victor's crinkled face lapsed into a smile. "You understand that he's simply following his superior's orders? That it isn't just Beeton who retains an interest in you…It's a department of Her Majesty's government, an intelligence department…Have you spoken with his employer yet – a Mr. Cage?"

Douglas shook his head, "Doesn't ring a bell, I'm afraid."

A slight smile tugged at Victor's mouth, "Well, I'm sure you will eventually, Mr. Salter. Despite everything, fate has an interesting way of interceding in these things."

The reporter frowned, unsure where this conversation was going, "I'm really not sure what you're getting at…"

"Do you mind?" asked Victor, helping himself to a scone. He licked at the cream and said, "Tell me, Mr. Salter, what exactly do you remember about your childhood?"

Douglas scowled irritably, "Do we know each other?" he countered, feeling suddenly wary. There was something about this man that made him unsure, but oddly he couldn't sense anything from him.

Victor smiled regretfully, "I suppose that there's no other way to go about this. Please accept my apologies beforehand."

Douglas shook his head with bewilderment,

"What on earth do you mean?" The furrows in Victor's brow deepened as he closed his eyes and appeared to sink into a meditative state.

Don't be afraid, he won't harm you, he's here to help, sang the familiar voice of Beatrice in the reporter's mind. Stunned by her intervention, he sank back into his chair, his eyes closed. The sights and feelings began slowly with a trickle. Soon enough, they rushed into a torrent as Victor shared his memories with the reporter.

Transfixed by the ongoing encounter between them, Janice looked from Douglas' face to Victor's with a growing sense of alarm. She could make out a barely perceptible hum, which appeared to emanate from deep within Victor's throat. "Is everything alright?" she whispered, taking Douglas's hand in her own.

He didn't reply, the reporter couldn't of even if he'd wanted to. He was lost in a fog of half-forgotten memories which intertwined with his own. His heart raced, and his breathing quickened as he recognised faces and places from his past.

Familiar smells and sounds drove home the fact that he was starting to recount and share his own memories with the stranger who'd sat down with them. *Lad, I'm a friend, not a stranger,* Victor's voice intoned soundlessly in the reporter's overwhelmed mind.

As he digested what he was told, Douglas saw himself as a young boy. He saw Victor as well, a little older than he was. They were walking somewhere together at night in some sort of procession. He shivered, feeling the cold air around them and Douglas could hear a haunting chant sounding as they marched.

Douglas shivered again as he caught sight of another familiar face. A spindly figure wrapped in a blood red robe. The reporter recoiled as he watched a younger Victor being tossed into a deep and murky body of water. "Oh my god!" he gasped aloud as he saw a scaly worm-like torso rising from the depths.

The mysterious figure sitting across from them broke the spell suddenly, and he grabbed tightly at the reporter's wrist. Douglas stared incredulously at him. "What the hell was that?"

Victor slid open his jacket and raised his shirt. A sizeable portion of his midriff was missing, as though something had taken a large bite out of him. "Aye, well that beastie managed a few nips before I escaped it."

Worriedly, Janice looked from Victor to Douglas, "What's going on?" she demanded.

"We appear to know each other," replied Douglas, his voice cracking. Overwhelmed, he stared searchingly into Victor's face, "We do—don't we?"

Victor patted his hand sympathetically, "We do lad," he replied after a long pause. "It's been a long time though." He returned his attention to the scone he'd been eating. "It's a lovely scone this," he murmured distractedly.

Speechless, Douglas slumped back into his chair, his face drained and his hair matted with sweat. After what seemed like ages, he finally said, "I've seen him recently, Makepeace. That bastard wanted me to join him."

Victor nodded as he chewed on the last of his scone, "I know, Douglas, I saw it all. You're a brave soul, standing up to him like that. He's far more powerful now than he ever was when we were kids." The reporter nodded uncertainly, not knowing how to respond. "That's why I'm here," continued Victor. "You can't face him alone lad, he's too strong. But together, we might just stand a chance."

"A chance?" asked Douglas warily.

Victor grinned, and it seemed to take years off him. "I've waited a long time for an opportunity like this, Douglas. You and I have the chance to right a wrong. We can do something that no one else can. We can stop him before it's too late."

Shaking his head, Douglas replied, "What the hell are you talking about? That man operates with impunity. He's working for the state, the government, as we speak."

"They're working for him," corrected Victor, holding up a finger to emphasise his point. The furrow in his brow grew deeper, "If he's successful in what he wants to achieve, the world will never recover. He'll be unopposed and all-powerful. Nothing will be able to stop him. It's now or never Douglas, only our working together can save the future."

Chilled to the bone by his words, the reporter felt sick to his stomach. "You're being serious? It's now or never?" he repeated anxiously.

Listen to Victor's words, Beatrice implored. *You must put a stop to Makepeace, before it's too late.*
Victor nodded in agreement, "Listen to Beatrice," he advised. She knows what she's talking about.

"You can hear her?" asked Douglas incredulously. Janice looked in bewilderment from the reporter to the odd Scot who'd taken an uninvited seat at their table.

He nodded, "But only when she speaks directly to you," replied Victor softly. "And I have to be nearby to hear her. Beatrice chose you because she knew that you could help. That you could avenge what was done to her and her children."

White with shock, the reporter felt a tear rolling down his cheek. "I'm not losing my mind?"

Victor cackled and broke into a broad smile, "No more than anyone else, Douglas. In fact, given what you've just learnt about yourself and by the way you've handled it, you're probably one of the sanest people I've met."

Douglas nodded, "It's all so overwhelming. What is it exactly that you want me to do?"

Grinning, Victor replied, "Well, I think the first thing we should do is order some more scones because they're delicious. And then I was hoping to speak with that detective friend of yours, Miss Scott?"

"I can arrange that," volunteered Janice brightly.

"I hoped you could," Victor replied, topping up their tea cups from the pot. He held his cup aloft, "A toast to victory," he announced, grinning from ear to ear like a deranged Cheshire cat.

Janice and Douglas looked briefly at one other and then clinked their tea cups against his in unison. "In for a penny, in for a pound," Janice agreed enthusiastically. Douglas didn't say a word, he was already starting to worry about what he'd just agreed to.

FORTY-SEVEN

The clock in the hallway ticked loudly, ominously, thought the Chief Science Advisor. Ticking round, the sound gave William Russell butterflies. He could almost feel them fluttering in his stomach. "You really don't have to come with me," he said.

"Nonsense," replied the detective, gripping his hand tightly. "I have to find out what's been happening to poor Mr. Salter. And from what you've told me, this chap, Harold Cage, could help to fill in some of the gaps."

Russell was already regretting what he'd shared with her. It was likely a breach of his security oath and he could already see his enforced retirement looming—if he even made it that far. One never really knew where one stood when Cage was involved. He shuddered at the thought and then glimpsed the Defence Chief ahead, waiting for them outside his office door. "Let me do the talking," he whispered, squeezing the detective's hand more tightly than he'd intended.

Velma squeezed back and nodded as they

approached the waiting figure of Harold Cage. Wordlessly, the Defence Chief opened the door to his office and pointedly invited his guests inside. "I know of someone who is absolutely desperate to meet you Bill, and also your friend, Miss Scott. Please do come inside whilst we all get acquainted."

Russell looked anxiously over at Velma. It was highly unusual for the Defence Chief to act like this; he was being almost pleasant. Suspiciously, he glanced at him before they entered, but Cage seemed to be lost in a world of his own. Alarms ringing internally, Russell took a deep breath and strode purposely into the Defence Chief's office.

"At last Mr. Russell, Miss Scott as well…what a delight to finally make your acquaintance." Makepeace casually lifted his polished brogues off of Cage's desk and dazzled them with his most winning of smiles. "Please do take a seat, both of you. I've so been looking forward to meeting you."

Russell looked anxiously over his shoulder at the Defence Chief. He couldn't quite believe what he'd just seen. Was Cage actually going to tolerate that? In his own office? "Oh we're the dearest of friends, aren't we Harold?" interjected Makepeace swiftly, as if he'd read Russell's thoughts.

"Please don't let us dally," he said as he pulled out chairs for them both. "Shall I be mother?" he offered brightly, not waiting for a response and already pouring tea into three delicate china cups, which sat on a silver tray. He made a shooing motion towards the Defence Chief, "Will you close the door on your way out please, Harold?"

Wordlessly, the Defence Chief nodded and bowed slightly before backing out of his own office. The heavy wooden door clicked shut behind them, and they found themselves sitting face-to-face with an earnest-looking Mr. Makepeace. "Well isn't this an unexpected treat?" he said, looking at them both searchingly. "The name's Makepeace, perhaps you've heard mention of me?"

Russell turned to look at Velma, whose gaze remained fixed on the figure sat opposite them. Eventually, the Science Chief shrugged and replied, "Not by name, sir, if I recall correctly. I presume Mr. Makepeace that you're the chap who Mr. Cage briefly mentioned to me. Although, I have to admit that I'm at a bit of a loss as to what's going on here. A little mystified even…"

The spindly figure nodded, "I dare say you are, Mr. Russell. Not you though, Miss Scott? You appear to know exactly what's going on here. I commend you on your powers of deduction."

She didn't reply, instead the detective was silently singing to herself over and over. Velma could only remember the first verse, but that didn't deter her; she just continued to repeat it.

"Really Miss Scott, you're going to persist with the 'Pirates of Penzance?'" Makepeace asked, a smirk playing on his lips. All pretence dropped from his countenance, he fixated on her, staring closely.

Flustered, Russell interjected, "Now you look here Mr. Makepeace, what exactly is going on?"

"Feeling a little left out of the loop are we, Mr. Russell?" mocked Makepeace. "I appreciate that it's a rather unusual experience. Almost rude one might say, and what are *your* thoughts, Miss Scott?"

Undeterred, she didn't reply, neither did she hesitate, the detective persisted with the words in her mind, *For I am a Pirate King!* A cruel smile crossed Makepeace's mouth, "I do find it rather amusing that you think that'll help you, Miss Scott."

Russell stood up abruptly, knocking over his chair in the process. The commotion broke the hypnotic spell that Velma was falling under, and Makepeace shot the Science Chief a cold, venomous look. "Cage was right about you Russell, you really are a buffoon." He shifted his focus towards him, seizing control of the Science Chief's body and forcing him to pick up the chair. "Now sit down," he scolded.

In that moment of distraction, Velma launched herself towards the tray perched on the desk. She flung it at Makepeace, the scalding tea arching through the air in his direction. The detective didn't even wait to see if it hit the mark, grabbing Russell by the hand, she urged them towards the office door, the only exit in the room.

Velma found herself suddenly stopped just short of the handle. Unwillingly, she turned around and looked on in horror as the tray of hot drinks slowly came to rest back down on the desk as if nothing had happened.

With a flick of his fingers, Velma and Bill found themselves marching unwillingly back towards their waiting chairs. "Shall we start again?" Makepeace suggested in a calm tone, which was betrayed by the look of pure malevolence that crossed his face.

Unable to resist, the detective and the Chief Science Advisor reluctantly sat back down. A sense of dread pervaded the room as Makepeace asked sharply, "Now then, where were we?"

FORTY-EIGHT

Janice shook her head, "The phone just keeps ringing. She's not there Douglas, do you think she's out somewhere with Mr. Russell?"

Shrugging, the reporter turned to look at Victor. "What do you suggest now?" Douglas watched with a bemused expression as the Scott placed an array of objects on the table in front of them.

"Now, what can you see?" he asked, staring at the reporter intensely.

"Well…" Douglas replied, "I can see a half-drunk mug of tea, a glass of water, a fork, a spoon, and a potted plant."

"Very good," replied Victor, standing up and making his way around the table. "Do you mind?" he asked Janice and, without waiting for a reply, he swiped the scarf from around her neck in a theatrical fashion. Victor bowed slightly in thanks and turned his attention back to the reporter.

"I want you to blindfold yourself, Douglas," he

said, handing him Janice's green scarf. "Please make sure it's secure and that you can't see through it." The reporter took the scarf and looked doubtfully over at Janice, who grinned back at him encouragingly. "Snap to it," pressed Victor, "we've no time to lose."

Nodding, the reporter followed the Scott's instructions, and secured the scarf around his head and over his eyes. "Now what?" he asked.

A rustle of noise followed and then Victor replied, "Look closely at the table again, I've removed some of the objects. Tell me what you can see now."

Douglas laughed, "I can't see a damn thing with this thing over my eyes."

"Try harder," insisted Victor. "The fact that your eyes are covered doesn't mean that you can't see. Remember, Beatrice has passed over and hasn't physically any eyes to speak of, and yet she's helped you on more than one occasion."

"Sounds like bloody nonsense," Douglas muttered testily. "If I can't see, how can I tell you what's there?"

Ignoring the irritable tone in the reporter's voice, Victor patiently replied, "Perhaps if you attempted it, you might find that you surprise yourself."

Sighing loudly, the reporter tried to focus on the task at hand. He stared ahead, dismissing the blackness that obscured his vision, and instead tried to focus on the individual threads of Janice's green scarf. As his concentration deepened, the hum of the traffic outside and the steady ticking of the clock in the room passed quietly into oblivion. Gradually, Douglas began to believe that he was starting to make some progress.

"Well?" Victor interrupted, "What can you see now?"

The reporter fought the urge to respond with a few choice words and instead held his tongue. As he did so, he began to make out the distinct shapes of the objects laid out on the table. "Bloody hell," he muttered aloud, more to himself than to anyone present in the room. "A spoon and a pepper grinder?" he announced uncertainly. "And a vase of flowers, carnations I think," he said with a growing sense of confidence.

"What colour?" asked Victor, his voice sounding incredibly distant.

"They're pink," the reporter replied, nodding his head as if to emphasise the fact.

Janice held her hand over her mouth, both shocked and surprised, as Victor replied, "That's very good, Douglas. Now, I want you to try and lift the carnations from the vase using only your mind."

"How exactly do I do that?" Douglas asked, no longer feeling as sceptical as he once had.

Victor winked at Janice, who'd taken to the sofa and continued to watch the proceedings with an equal measure of awe and unease. "Douglas, just reach out to it in the same way you would as if you were using your hands. Reach out and grab hold of it."

The reporter nodded and focused on the blurry outline of the flowers resting in the vase. He reached out tentatively and tried to take hold of them. There was no familiar sense of touch or any sign that he'd made any kind of contact with them. Douglas tried again and attempted to coax the carnations out of the vase and up into the air.

He sighed with frustration as they removed to budge. "Again," Victor urged, "you're close, I can sense it."

Douglas redoubled his efforts, Victor's words of encouragement ringing in his ears. This time, he didn't try a tactile approach; instead, he simply willed himself to take hold of them. Through the blindfold, he thought he saw the flowers begin to levitate up and out of the vase. He slowly twisted them about, in mid-air, this way and that. "You're doing it, Douglas!" Janice squealed excitedly. The interruption caused Douglas to lose his focus and the carnations floated soundlessly to the floor.

The reporter tore the blindfold from his eyes, blinking unsteadily as he adjusted to the light, and took in Janice's and Victor's contrasting facial expressions. Incredulously, he stared at the flowers still lying prostrate on the floor and then back up at Victor, who nodded and grinned wolfishly.

Douglas focused on the carnations and again caused them to lift. They spun wildly in the air without him laying a finger on them. He carefully manoeuvred the flowers back into the vase, exerting much more control than he had the first time. Smiling with satisfaction, the reporter chuckled and winked at Victor. "It's incredible," he muttered distractedly.

The Scott smiled patiently, "We've a lot to do and not much time. Take a short break and then we'll start again." Victor looked over at the clock, "Shall we say a quarter hour from now?"

The reporter nodded, "Yes, I could do with a drink in the meantime."

"Don't drink anything alcoholic, it'll impair the

process, and you're not yet in control of the ability. You'll also find that performing this will tend to make you feel dehydrated. So, make sure that you drink plenty of fluids, regularly and throughout the day."

"Is there anything else?" asked Douglas, making a mental note of Victor's advice.

"Yes," he replied, "but it can keep until we complete the next session. Go and grab yourself some fresh air, you'll find it restorative and I think, worthwhile…"

***

Douglas gripped Janice's hand tightly as they stepped outside. He took a deep breath and took in the colours which seemed somehow brighter. Bird songs followed them as they walked, it sounded almost orchestral to him. The reporter giggled exuberantly, he felt giddy, a bit drunk even. "Are you alright?" asked Janice, concern showing on her face.

The reporter nodded enthusiastically, "I'm better than alright Janice. In fact, I'm feeling bloody marvelous." Grinning boyishly, he pecked her on the cheek. "I don't know how to explain it; it's as if I'm seeing things for the first time as if I'd just been born."

Janice stopped them in the street and shook her head, "I'm worried about you Douglas."

He laughed impishly, "There's nothing to worry about. It's fine, Janice. I'm fine, you're fine, and soon this will all be over, and we'll all be fine." She scrutinised his face carefully, looking for a sign that things were not as they seemed. He continued to beam at her, his grin widening the closer she looked. He patted her hand reassuringly, "It's all fine, I promise you," he said, trying to reassure her. Reluctantly, Janice nodded, and they made their way back to the detective's office where Victor was waiting for them.

FORTY-NINE

Velma moaned, she felt as if she'd just been hit by a bus. Her head was pounding and her vision blurry; it felt like the worst hangover of all time. She looked over to her left and found William Russell slumped in the chair next to hers. "Bill—wake up!" she urged, shaking him, "Wake up!" But William Russell refused to stir, despite her promptings.

Groggily, she stood up. They were still in Harold Cage's office, and aside from themselves, it was completely deserted. Her legs felt heavy as she cautiously made her way over to the door and tried the handle; it was locked from the outside. "Damn," she hissed, wondering whether or not to pound against the sturdy wooden panelling. *Surely someone will hear me*, she thought. But who that someone might be, prevented her from hammering urgently against it. She didn't fancy a second round with Makepeace and wasn't sure if she'd be up for it any time in the foreseeable future.

"Velma?" croaked a voice.

She turned and found an ashen-faced William Russell looking over at her. "What happened?" he asked, grimacing.

Velma realised that he already knew, but was just too scared to admit it. "Makepeace happened," she replied simply.

He nodded. "I'd really hoped that it wasn't true. So what now?" he rasped, sounding forlorn, resigned almost.

Velma didn't immediately respond, this was one of those rare occasions where she wasn't quite sure what to do. Forcing herself to focus, she eventually settled on the fire alarm switch bolted to the wall of the Defence Chief's office. A sly smile crossed her face as a plan started to formulate. "Don't you worry Bill—I've got an idea." *Or at least, I hope I have*, she thought to herself, but didn't dare say aloud.

***

Janice lay flat on the floor of the detective's office. She suppressed an urge to squeal as she felt herself slowly rising off the floor. "Carefully now," urged Victor, watching as Douglas frowned with concentration. He delicately manoeuvred Janice's prostrate figure towards the sofa. "That's it lad, now plop her down, gently."

Breathing with exertion, the reporter slowly let her figure come to rest on top of the cushioned sofa. He let out a sigh of relief, which was mirrored by Janice, as she felt herself gain control over her own movements.

Victor nodded patiently, "Now Janice, I want you to think back to your earliest childhood memory. Try and recall it, and then I want you to focus on that and nothing else. Are you ready?" She nodded nervously, "Right then, Douglas, try and sense what she's thinking. It might be an image, a sound, maybe even a feeling. Just try and get a sense of what it is. Be kind though, don't just go barging in; her mind and her memories are private things."

The reporter nodded and gently began to try and sense what was on Janice's mind. "I think I can smell cake," he murmured through half-closed eyes, his senses straining, "Chocolate cake?"

Janice nodded, her eyes wide like saucers. "I remembered baking with my grandmother, when I was around four years old. She used to let me lick the bowl," Janice said with a fond smile as she recalled the cherished memory.

The reporter smiled wistfully, "I could almost taste it, Janice. I sensed that you were close and that you loved her very much."

Wiping a small tear from her eye, she smiled sweetly. "I did Douglas, I really did."

The moment they were sharing was broken by Victor sharply clapping his hands together. "I'm afraid that we're out of time, Douglas. It's time to go. We can't wait any longer before we face him."

"Now?" asked the reporter with astonishment. "I don't even know what I'm doing yet."

Victor sighed as though he were agreeing with him, "Your friend, the detective, needs our assistance. Makepeace has her, and she won't escape unscathed without help. We have to go now, before it's too late."

Douglas switched his gaze from Janice's panic-stricken face to the craggy-featured Scott on the opposite side of the room. Trying to suppress his fear and nagging sense of doubt, he replied, "Well, if she's in trouble, I suppose we should go and help. I wouldn't want her to face that monster alone."

"I'll come with you," volunteered Janice, leaping up from the sofa.

"I don't think that's a good idea," replied Victor. "Makepeace will sense Douglas's feelings towards you and try to take advantage of them. It's best if you stay here. It'll be safer for everyone."

Sullenly, she nodded and sat back down, feeling excluded. "Besides," added Victor, "I have an important task for you in mind. And we won't succeed without your assistance."

"You do?" she asked, brightening.

The Scott nodded and scrawled a phone number on a scrap of paper. "Precisely forty-five minutes from now, I want you to call this number. It'll put you through to our mutual acquaintance, Mr. Beeton. Tell him who you are and that I've asked you to relay an important message to him."

"What's the message?" asked Janice.

"Tell him that his employer, Mr. Cage, has been unduly influenced. Tell him that if he really wants to serve his country, he'll come alone and meet me and Douglas an hour from now, outside his place of work. Tell him, Janice, that he'll need to come armed."

She nodded, her face pale and taut, "Anything else?" she asked nervously.

He half smiled, "We'll meet outside Parliament

at half past five exactly, just by the banks of the Thames. Why don't you come and join us, once all this is resolved. I'm sure Douglas would like that, Velma too."

Janice grinned enthusiastically, "Alright, Victor, I will. You said half past five?"

Victor winked at her mischievously, "But not a moment earlier," he said, raising a finger in warning. "Promise me!"

Janice nodded and hurriedly gave Douglas a hug. "Be careful," she called after them as they descended the staircase, one after another. Bolting the door shut after they left, she looked over at the phone on her desk and then over at the clock. *Half past five*, she mouthed under her breath.

***

Beeton hung up the phone, a glazed expression fixed on his face. He reached into his desk drawer and removed his service revolver. Carefully, he stripped it down and oiled it before placing it securely in his holster. Throughout the ritual, the intelligence officer remained steadfast, seemingly locked into some sort of trance. A commotion outside in the corridor suddenly broke the spell and he leapt up urgently from behind his chair.

The sound of the fire alarm rang through the corridors of Whitehall with an unrelenting finality. "That racket's loud enough to raise the dead," muttered Russell, placing his hands over his ears to try and stem the assault on his senses.

"That's the idea," replied Velma, who began banging urgently on the door to Harold Cage's office.

She heard the pounding of footsteps rushing past and bellowed, "Open the bloody door!" The footsteps came to a halt somewhere outside, and she hammered against the door again, "We're locked in…"

She stepped back, feeling suddenly apprehensive as the door handle turned. "It's locked," announced a gruff voice from the other side.

"Beeton?" asked Russell, recognising the man's voice, "Is that you?"

"Mr. Russell?" replied the voice, sounding surprised. "What are you doing in there? And where's Mr. Cage?" he added, suddenly suspicious.

"Never mind that," snapped Russell. "Can't you hear the bloody fire alarm ringing? We're trapped in here. Get the damn door open!"

The intelligence officer agonised over the decision. Surely the Defence Chief had locked Russell in there for a good reason. Still, with the fire alarm ringing, he couldn't very well leave him to burn. And the call he'd just received from the detective's secretary had shaken him. For some reason, his encounter up in Scotland had flashed before his eyes as she'd spoken, and it had shaken him to the very core of his being. "Who's in there with you?" he asked, still wrestling with whether to do as he was being instructed.

"Miss Scott's in here with me," declared Russell agitatedly. "Listen to me Beeton, Cage is not thinking straight right now. He's somehow been influenced by that rogue Makepeace, he's the one who's locked us both in here."

Beeton relented, that did actually make some sort of sense. He'd been swayed himself by the power that

Makepeace seemed to possess right up until Janice had spoken to him. The memory of seeing his own death play out was not something he wanted to dwell on. And despite his yearning to learn more from Makepeace about *The Knowledge*, he made up his mind. "I'll get you out of there," he agreed, rattling the door handle again.

It didn't give and instead, he shoved at it with his shoulder, but the door was old and heavy, and the lock which held it in place was secure. "Step away from the door," he ordered sharply, reaching for his revolver.

Velma and Russell leapt back as a hail of bullets suddenly tore against the sturdy, brass lock on the heavy, ancient door. The door handle turned again, and finally, there was a click. The latch lifted.

The Chief Science Advisor beamed at the detective, "You're quite marvellous, you know."

Blushing slightly, Velma pecked him on the cheek as Beeton crashed through the splintered door. "Well done, Beeton," Russell cried enthusiastically, pumping the surprised man's hand up and down. "Now, let's get out of here whilst we still can."

They raced through the maze of corridors and down the flights of stairs until they emerged breathlessly from the realm of Whitehall and out into the open air. "I'm so glad that you managed to join us," declared a voice, which made all of them turn in unison.

In a state of confusion, Beeton held his ground unsure how to react. It was as if he was torn between two worlds. He forced himself to look at his watch, which read five-forty, as Russell groaned loudly and Velma hissed the name, "Makepeace."

FIFTY

Victor and Douglas loitered by the street corner as they watched the detective, the Chief Science Advisor, and the intelligence officer being marched away from Whitehall. "We're too late," lamented the reporter.

"Not at all," replied Victor calmly. "In fact, we're right on time. Follow me…" Douglas hurried after him as Victor began to take long strides, keeping the quarry on the opposite side of the road just within sight.

"He knows you're nearby," Victor muttered, glancing over at the reporter. "Go after them, I'll take a different route and meet you outside the Parliament building. Try and steer them towards the banks of the Thames."

"How do I do that?" demanded Douglas anxiously.

The Scott grinned at him, "Use your ability to place obstacles in their path, people, cars, lorries… Whatever you can. Force them to take the path you want." Douglas paused uncertainly as the figures began to grow distant. "Lad, you can do it," encouraged Victor. "Have a little faith in yourself."

Despite his growing sense of unease, Douglas nodded in agreement. Holding on to his hat, the reporter dashed across the road, chasing down the small group ahead. They appeared to have slowed, and he desperately hurried after them whilst trying to calculate the necessary twists and turns required to force them onto the banks of the Thames, just outside of the Parliament building.

Stay back a little, you're getting too close, warned Beatrice. Douglas obeyed and slackened his pace whilst maintaining a steely gaze on those ahead. *He's toying with you,* she whispered furiously. *Give him a taste of his own medicine.*

"How?" he replied, his voice cracking and his throat dry with apprehension.

Do you see the protestors on the bridge? Steer them into his path, he won't want to lose his hostages. The reporter struggled to influence and move the throng from the centre of the road to the pavement on the right-hand side. *Don't try and move them all,* advised Beatrice, *just the ones at the front of the line, the rest will simply follow.*

The reporter smiled as he obeyed her advice, and he watched almost incredulously as the swarm of people moved into the path of his prey. His smile widened as he heard Makepeace barking orders at a clearly confused Beeton for him to keep tabs on Velma Scott and William Russell.

Douglas laughed as his targets crossed the road onto the far side, just as he'd intended. His confidence soaring, the reporter moved the protestors back into the middle of the road, and he boxed his targets in, ensuring they jostled into one another.

He was growing more accustomed to using his gift, and it seemed to be becoming almost instinctive. The reporter's eyes narrowed as he closed in on Makepeace. And he took a great deal of satisfaction from the fact that he'd inconvenienced him after their previous encounter.

Beeton shook his head and refused as Makepeace barked another set of orders at him. Raging, the gangly figure effortlessly pushed him aside and glared furiously at Douglas Salter. Increasing his pace, the reporter closed in on them, the crowds dispersing before him like the waters of the Red Sea when parted by Moses. He could sense the animosity emanating from Makepeace as the distance closed between them; he reciprocated in turn.

Beeton remained seated on the pavement in a state of shock. He'd heard the command from Makepeace to act but had been unable to comply. Another voice was present within his mind. A voice that overwhelmed him, he recognised its Scottish brogue, *Victor*, he finally realised. As it dawned on him who was speaking, the vision he'd experienced back in Scotland of his own demise flashed before his eyes again, and he shuddered with fright.

"Stand up and fight," barked Makepeace furiously and forced the intelligence officer to pull out his pistol. Unwillingly, Beeton reached into his jacket, his hand shaking. A sly smile crossed Makepeace's face as he regained some control, and he roughly wrapped his forearm around Velma's throat and backed slowly away, holding her in front of him like a shield.

The din of the protesters seemed to fall away as Douglas and Makepeace began to circle one another like ancient warriors poised to do battle. "Do something!" pleaded Russell desperately, grabbing hold of Beeton's arm. Sweat poured down the intelligence officer's brow as he wavered, his aim switching between Makepeace and the reporter. "Please don't let him hurt her," begged Russell, "I love her."

Beeton's finger squeezed the trigger, and three shots rang out in quick succession. Harmlessly, the bullets glanced off the road. He squeezed again and missed twice more, a single bullet remaining loaded in his firearm. "What are you doing?" raged Makepeace, stealing a glance towards him.

Douglas took advantage of the split-second distraction and grabbed hold of Velma's arm. Already sensing his movement, the detective balled her opposite hand into a fist. She slammed it down violently into Makepeace's groin, before grabbing hold and twisting and turning. He grunted with pain and his arm slipped from around her throat. She spun around and slapped him hard across the face, leaving a palm-shaped welt on his face. Douglas dragged desperately at her other arm, urging her away.

Velma held firm and aimed a sharp kick at Makepeace's shin, which elicited a yelp of surprised pain before Douglas managed to manoeuvre himself between the pair. Douglas caught the spindly figure, with a swift right hook and Makepeace stumbled backwards with a look of complete shock etched onto his face.

The look turned to one of fear when he noticed Beeton's sidearm was now pointing his weapon directly at him. "It's been a long time," announced a Scottish voice as

Victor stepped into view, "far too long."

"Victor?" Makepeace hissed incredulously. "It's not possible, I watched you die." Slowly, Makepeace began to edge back as they advanced on his position. The realisation of what had happened, who had undermined his power, slowly dawned on him. Unused to feelings of fear, his heart was racing as he stumbled and fell backwards over a low wall that lined the walkway.

Hurriedly, he scrambled to his feet and backed further away, but like a pack of wolves, the group swarmed around him, waiting for the right moment to strike. Makepeace stood on the shores of the Thames, the water lapping at his ankles. Pleadingly, he held out a hand towards Douglas, "I should have known sooner that you couldn't have managed this alone. But it's not too late, we can still be there for one another, you and I Douglas—you are my child, my son."

A wave of nausea passed over the reporter as he heard the words. "You know it to be true," Makepeace spoke, making his final gambit.

Douglas shook his head, "My father died a long time ago."

"No, that's not true," refuted Makepeace. "Why do you think I could never bring myself to really harm you, even when you deserved it." The spittle flew from his lips, quickly and urgently. "Why do you think you possess these abilities? Victor knows it to be true, don't you? Tell him the truth boy, you are both my children."

FIFTY-ONE

Douglas glanced hesitantly over at Victor, unable to speak. The Scot simply nodded while Makepeace waded further back into the water, which had reached waist height. "Hold your position!" bellowed Beeton, aiming his weapon with the remaining bullet at the retreating figure. "I said hold your position," he ordered adamantly.

Velma broke free from the protective embrace that Russell was holding her in and placed her hand on the intelligence officer's arm. Slowly, he lowered the revolver, "This isn't for you to resolve," she spoke softly. He nodded as she spoke, realising the truth of her words.

"We could have remade the world, you and I," wailed Makepeace, a wild look haunting his eyes. "We still can, if you're willing to try. Douglas, what do you say?"

"Are you ready?" asked Victor, sounding as though he were seeking permission.

Veil-like, the London smog lifted momentarily, and Douglas spied a crowd of onlookers gawking from the bridge overlooking the murky river. "Ready for what?" he whispered hoarsely.

Victor maintained a watchful eye over the spindly figure still trying to make his escape. "Ready to end this tyrant's rule?" he replied, his voice far away, betraying no sign of remorse. "He must be stopped before it's too late. We'll never get a chance like this again."

Douglas Salter alternated his gaze, his focus shifting from his brother to his father. *You promised me*, chimed Beatrice's voice, from a realm somewhere beyond life and death itself. At a loss for words, the reporter grunted his agreement, uncertain as to what would follow. *Thank you, Douglas*, spoke Beatrice, with a finality that shook him.

Moribund, Douglas gasped as a churn of water suddenly raced towards the spindly figure, still trying to make his escape. "What's happening?" Douglas stammered uncertainly. Victor placed a reassuring arm around his shoulder and squeezed him affectionately.

"Something which should have happened a long time ago lad, we're simply closing the circle." Makepeace shrieked with fear, as a large, scaly mass brushed against his leg. Aghast, he stared into the water, and then as the realisation hit him, he caught Victor's eye and howled with fury. "Goodbye, father," whispered Victor, as the beast clamped its tooth-filled jaws around Makepeace's leg and dragged him violently beneath the water's surface.

Russell turned with shock towards Victor, "What the hell was that?"

Velma whistled loudly, "I'd really like to talk to you about this sometime, Victor."

Smiling cryptically, he replied, "That beastie and

I go a long way back. It has a taste for the flesh of those in our family." He turned back to look over the river as a few bubbles escaped to the top of the water. Sighing, he gently steered Douglas away from the shores of the Thames. "Come away from the water's edge. That beastie should have had its fill for one day, but one can never be too sure."

The reporter obeyed, too shocked to respond. "Besides, there's someone waiting for you," Victor spoke, pointing to Janice's silhouette as she rushed excitedly towards them. "If I were you, Douglas, I'd keep a hold of that one and make an honest woman of her."

The reporter looked over at his brother and blushed. "I, erm," he mumbled awkwardly as the sound of Janice's voice calling his name drew his attention. He smiled bashfully and then raced over to embrace her tightly as they met on the shore.

"Ahhh," remarked Velma fondly, squeezing Russell's hand. "That reminds me of something," she said, looking up at him brightly. "Up on the bridge, I'm sure I heard you say that you loved me. Isn't that right, Mr. Beeton? I'm sure I heard Mr. Russell say that."

The detective winked at the intelligence officer as William Russell turned a bright shade of pink. Beeton grinned lopsidedly at her and replied, "You know Miss Scott, I think you're right. I do seem to recall Mr. Russell saying something along those lines."

"It was simply the heat of the moment," blustered the government's Chief Science Advisor as they headed back up away from the shore and towards the road and the startled onlookers. "Besides, who in their right mind would say such a thing after just one date?"

"Oh that's definitely you alright," teased Douglas, unable to resist. "I knew as soon as I saw you both together that you were in trouble, Mr. Russell. I suspect Miss Scott knew that too."

William Russell frowned at Velma, "Yes, well, about that time we first met. You told me that poor Mr. Salter here had been following you. You asked me to step in and save you, if I recall."

Douglas and Janice grinned, "She did say that you know," agreed the reporter, chuckling.

"A woman has her ways, Bill," remarked Velma cheerily. "Otherwise, nothing would ever get done, would it?" And with that, she grabbed him by the lapel of his jacket and planted a large, wet kiss on his lips.

Turning an even deeper shade of pink, Russell began to laugh. "Who am I to argue with the mighty Velma Scott?"

Folding her arms across her chest, she replied matter of factly, "Well those are my thoughts exactly."

FIFTY-TWO

arold Cage, the Defence Chief, folded the newspaper in two and then snorted derisively. "Is this some sort of joke?" He looked expectantly at the small group hovering around his desk. Velma helped herself to a large brandy from the tray in his office and chose to ignore the scowl he flashed in her direction. Instead, she emptied the bottle and began handing around glasses to those assembled.

"No, sir," replied Beeton. "As you can see for yourself, there were multiple witnesses to Makepeace's death."

"This rubbish is tabloid stuff," growled Cage. "This is not an official report, and it's hardly likely to be sanctioned as the official government record."

"And yet, that's exactly what happened," replied Russell calmly. He clinked his glass against Velma's and took a satisfyingly large glug of the Defence Chief's brandy.

"We all witnessed it," agreed Douglas Salter, playfully squeezing Janice's arm as he sank into the armchair by the fireplace and closed his eyes.

Cage glared at them frostily and then turned his attention to Beeton. "Write something up for the official record. Make sure you sign the thing, and I'll actively consider not firing you."

The intelligence officer reached inside his jacket and placed a sealed envelope in the Defence Chief's hand. "That's my letter of resignation, sir. I'm afraid you'll have to find someone else to write up your report."

Unaccustomed to an act of what he considered to be unadulterated defiance from one of his agents, the Defence Chief paled. "Resignation?" He laughed cruelly, "You don't actually think you're qualified for any other type of employment do you?"

"He's going to join my detective agency," Velma announced brightly. "We've already signed the paperwork. Frank will be on board from Monday."

Cage shook his head and turned to William Russell, "Right then, Russell, you write it up."

The Chief Science Advisor grinned. "Actually, I'm retiring from the service, Harold. You see, I'm getting married. I'm afraid that you'll have to put your own name on the official record."

"Married?" spluttered Cage. "To who?" Velma slinked her arm through Russell's and winked at the Defence Chief. "So you're retiring as well, are you, Miss Scott?"

She chuckled, "Oh, no such luck. A woman has to retain her financial independence somehow, especially in this day and age." Cage looked at them all incredulously as they lounged around his office, helping themselves to his brandy.

Cheerily, they watched for the Defence Chief's reaction as his face began to change hue. Smiling and nudging one another, they remained tight-lipped as the clock in the office ticked loudly. Eventually, he gathered what remained of his composure and stood up abruptly. He grabbed at the newspaper on his desk and screwed it into a ball before launching it towards the waste basket.

He sighed deeply and finally said, "Well, I suppose that congratulations are in order then." He raised his glass towards his former intelligence officer. And then towards Russell and Velma. "Good luck to you all. And what about you Mr. Salter…are you moving on to new pastures as well?"

Douglas grinned, "Rather unexpectedly, I've just come into a small inheritance up in Scotland. Janice and I are going to take a look around. It turns out that I might have some family up there."

"I see," replied Cage. "Well, good luck to you both as well then." He bristled and then made his way over to his office door, holding it open for them. "I'm sure you'll appreciate that I'm a very busy man…so if you wouldn't mind…and please do close the door on your way out will you?"

Velma firmly placed her empty glass on Cage's desk and marched frostily towards him. She ushered him away from the door and slammed it shut. "We're not finished here yet, Harold. Your project has to be closed down. The work on the psychic resonator needs to stop. It's simply too dangerous to be allowed to exist," urged Velma.

Cage glared pointedly over at William Russell

before replying to Velma. "I don't know what you are talking about, my dear. There is no such project. Besides, I can't imagine that a man hoping to be married shortly would be so stupid as to commit treason and to publicly reveal the existence of a state secret." He looked over at William Russell again, as if to emphasise his point and underline it to the pair of them.

"Actually," replied Velma with a wicked grin, "you revealed its existence when you were under the influence of Mr. Makepeace."

"I did no such thing," growled Cage. "I was just playing along trying to get him to reveal his secrets. I was never under any kind of undue influence."

"My apologies, sir, but I have to say, that's not entirely true," interceded Beeton. "You see, I have a clear recollection of your rather odd behaviour during that period. So much so in fact, that I took the liberty of making a record of it. Dates and such like."

Cage scowled, "Blackmail—is that the right word for it, Beeton?"

Beeton shrugged innocently, "What can I say, sir, I learnt a lot under your tutelage." A long silence descended as Harold Cage assessed his options.

"I would of course back up Mr. Beeton's claim," volunteered William Russell helpfully. "Perhaps you should consider retirement yourself Harold? You've more than put in the time. Maybe it's an opportunity for a younger man to oversee things. You know, someone more attuned to the times."

Harold Cage glanced around the assembled faces in his office and finally relented. "Alright, alright, You have my word that the project will stop," he agreed.

Velma clapped her hands together delightedly. "Well, that's settled then. Can you put that in writing please, Harold? We will, of course, want to keep an eye on you, just to check that you're being true to your word."

The Defence Chief smiled craftily and grabbed a pen and paper from his desk. He wrote down the order to terminate the project and signed it with a flourish. With a sigh, he handed it over to Velma. "Satisfied?"

She looked over at Douglas, who casually scanned the Defence Chief's mind and then nodded. "He's telling the truth at the moment."

Cage paled and regarded Douglas Salter with a rising sense of horror. He recalled the same stunt being pulled by Makepeace. "You're one as well?"

Douglas grinned and winked at him, "Turns out there are a few of us about. And as Velma said, we'll be keeping a careful eye on you Harold. By the way, I'd appreciate it if you handed over the device and any blueprints to Mr. Beeton for safekeeping. I'm sure he's as keen as I am to see them destroyed."

The former intelligence officer nodded. "I'll see to it on the way out. That kind of thing should never see the light of day. It has the potential to destroy our very way of life. I understand the consequences almost better than anyone here, aside from Mr. Salter." They smiled at one another, a newfound understanding thawing their earlier mutual mistrust and dislike.

The detective laughed, "Of course Harold, you're more than welcome to attend our wedding. In fact, we wouldn't dream of you not attending, would we Bill? Do you have a best man in mind?"

William Russell shook his head and then burst into laughter. "Let's leave him be, love. As Harold said, he's a very busy man. And well, I don't know about you lot, but I'm absolutely parched." He glanced at his watch enthusiastically, "Besides, I do believe it's opening time at our favourite pub, my love."

Velma grinned, "Sounds like a perfect plan, Bill. Come on you lot, the first round is on me."

THE END

ACKNOWLEDGEMENTS

I'd like to thank everyone at 8th & Atlas Publishing for their support throughout. I really appreciated the feedback which Christina De Paris provided throughout the editing process, her insights were invaluable.

I'd also like to thank Breonna Rossi for her cover concept. She has (telepathically almost) brought what I had in my minds eye to life – amazing!

And lastly, I'd like to thank Michael De Paris whose patience and kind words of support and encouragement really helped me to get this over the finish line.

ABOUT THE AUTHOR

Alex is based in Manchester, UK and shares his life with his wife & cat. Alex is also the author of *The Courier* and *The Ghost in the Garden*.

Velma Scott & the Curious Case of the Telepathists

WRITTEN BY:
Alex Stivaros

8TH & ATLAS PUBLISHING